The Corpse
In Oozak's
Pond

The Corpse
In Oozak's
Pond

CHARLOTTE MACLEOD

THE MYSTERIOUS PRESS • New York

Copyright © 1987 by Charlotte MacLeod
All rights reserved.
The Mysterious Press, 129 West 56th Street, New York, N.Y. 10019

Printed in the United States of America
First Printing: April 1987
10 9 8 7 6 5 4 3 2 1

Library of Congress Cataloging in Publication Data

MacLeod, Charlotte.
  The corpse in Oozak's Pond.

  1. Title
PS3563.P31865C67   1987   813'.54   86-62775
ISBN 0-89296-188-0

326893

For Jean and Lou Steinberg

THE BUGGINS FAMILY IN BALACLAVA COUNTY*

Habakkuk Buggins 1759–1817

Abelard 1781–1845	Druella 1790–1862 m. Fortitude Lumpkin	Balaclava 1803–1892 m. Nausicaa Lomax

Corydon 1801–1877	Ichabod 1809–1874 m. Prudence Plover	Belial 1812–1882	Dalbert 1811–1878	Huxford 1827–1863

Knightsbridge 1843–1928

Augustus 1856–1904

Trevelyan 1902–1985 m. Beatrice Sill

Elwell 1889–1961 twice married

Bracebridge 1923 –	Bainbridge 1923 – ?	Persephone 1930 –	Boatwright 1921 –	Trowbridge 1923 –	Grace 1937 – m. Philip Porble

* This incomplete chart is intended solely to clarify relationships among family members mentioned in the accompanying narrative. For added genealogical data see THE BUGGINS FAMILY IN BALACLAVA COUNTY au. Helen Marsh Shandy DLS; pub. The Pied Pica Press, Clavaton, Mass.

The Corpse In Oozak's Pond

Chapter 1

> "'Oh, fell the deed and foul the play
> When he whose eye so fond
> Had erst beheld the gladsome day
> Turned up in Oozak's Pond.'"

Peter Shandy, professor of agronomy at Balaclava Agricultural College and aficionado of verse trying to pass itself off as poetry, rolled out the lines with unctuous fervor. Helen Shandy, curator of the Buggins Collection, sneezed as she opened yet another bundle of the Corydon Buggins Archive.

"Peter, darling, must you?"

"What do you mean, must I? Can't you appreciate the ineluctable god-awfulness of it? Listen:

> "'Tho' bravely did he struggle till
> The waters closed him o'er,
> Old Oozak soon his lungs did fill.
> Gus sank to th' oozy floor.'

"Since when was any Buggins ever named Gus?"

"Augustus Caesar Buggins, 1856–1904," Helen replied, sneezing again. "Oozak's Pond is nonsense, of course. There's no such place and never was."

"Fine words, forsooth! Here you are enjoying its benefits as you deny its very existence. Oozak's Pond, my love, is that oversize puddle up above the methane plant whence

1

cometh the water that turns the wheel that drives the shaft that squashes the ordure that releases the gas that lights the lamps at our august seat of learning, not to mention that lamp you're sneezing at right now."

The lamp was a nice old brass one. Helen gave its green glass shade a little pat of apology. "So that's a pond? I thought it was some kind of man-made reservoir. Ponds don't usually come with concrete rims, do they?"

"Oozak's didn't have one back when Balaclava Buggins's first freshman class led the college kine to slurp from its mossy banks."

"I thought they slurped from that other pond over by the animal husbandry department."

"Nay, my fair. That's where they slurp nowadays, when the mood is upon them and the pond isn't frozen over. That, however, is not the primal slurping ground. In fact, it's where our founder's wife used to do the students' wash."

"Aha," cried Helen. "Hence the name Wash Pond."

"Precisely. Mrs. Buggins's name was Nausicaa. Pronounced, no doubt, Nawsicker. The old cowsheds were where the methane plant is now. There used to be a conduit made from hollow logs running down from the pond to fill the drinking troughs for those cows who didn't care to make the climb to the pond. Legend has it that while cleaning out the trough one day, young Dalbert Buggins conceived the notion of harnessing the water power from Oozak's Pond to run a gristmill. At one time, Oozak's Pond ground all the college flour. As time went on and technology became more complex, the mill became the power plant, but Oozak's Pond still burbles on in the same old way."

"Dalbert." Helen studied her still incomplete genealogy chart. "I have him. He was Balaclava's nephew—not his son as is popularly supposed. Balaclava's only son, Huxford, was killed in the Civil War."

"Yes, and Huxford's cousin Corydon almost brast a gut trying to think up a rhyme for Chickamauga so he could pen the memorial ode. Speaking of the Buggins bard and his odes, where was I?"

"Somewhere odious, no doubt. Shouldn't we just be resting quietly so we'll be fresh for the Groundhog Day ceremony tomorrow morning? I hope the little beast will have the decency not to see his shadow this time. Last year he gave us an extra six weeks of winter."

Helen sneezed again with scholarly resignation. After all, she'd brought this dust upon herself. Six months ago, she'd presented a paper on Corydon Buggins's brother Belial at a symposium in Arizona. The stir she'd created in academic circles had spurred President Thorkjeld Svenson to demand from her a definitive history of Balaclava and all the attendant Bugginses.

They'd been a family of writers and savers. She had plenty of material to work with; her trouble came in getting down to it. As a member of the college library staff, she was still subject to constant interruption from Librarian Philip Porble and his minions. Helen had quit trying to work in the Buggins Room and begun lugging armloads of ana back to the small brick house on the Crescent below the campus that she shared with Shandy and their cat, Jane Austen.

This had necessitated turning the upstairs guest room into a sort of den-cum-office. The downstairs cubbyhole Shandy had been using for grading papers and suchlike ever since his bachelor days was really too small for one, let alone two; although neither of the Shandys was a large person. They'd talked of building on an additional room, but February was no time to begin tearing down walls. February wasn't a propitious time for much of anything in Balaclava County, Massachusetts. That was why Groundhog Day, February 2, had grown to loom so large on the college calendar.

Naturally, President Svenson wasn't going to accept any secondhand prognostication from Punxsatawney Pete or Cochituate Chuck. Balaclava Beauregard was already snoozing in the wings, or, more properly, in a hole up on the bank of what Helen now knew to be Oozak's Pond. On the dot of half past six the next morning, the grumpy woodchuck would be hauled out of his snug den and set on a platform of snow that had been stamped down hard for his meteorological convenience.

Truth to tell, Beauregard probably wouldn't see his shadow no matter what the weather because he wouldn't bother to open his eyes, woodchucks being among the most determined hibernators of all Mammalia. That didn't amount to a hill of beans. The entire student body, most of the faculty, their families, and a goodly number of townsfolk would be on hand to help him look for it.

Once the Official Groundhog Shadow Viewer had examined the evidence and pronounced the prognostication, Beauregard would go back to bed. A bonfire would be lighted; hot cocoa and crullers would be dispensed to the cheering multitudes from a big sled drawn by four magnificent Balaclava Blacks. The horses, well blanketed against the chill, would be stamping and snorting, jingling their harness bells, and having a bait of oats so they wouldn't feel left out and no misguided freshman would start feeding them crullers in defiance of the strict dietary rules for college livestock set down by Professor Daniel Stott of the animal husbandry department.

As for the students, of course, they'd eat everything in sight and thrive on it. They'd sing college songs and stage snowball fights, then they'd roll up great masses of snow to build an effigy of Old Man Winter. Finally, they'd topple the snowman into the bonfire, the fire would go out, and the fun would be over. The horses would pull the sled back to the barn; the students would run after to boost it over the ruts, then they'd scatter to classes and another day's work.

A silly business, no doubt, but Shandy wouldn't have missed it for anything. Nor would Helen. She'd been promised a place of honor on the sled, helping her dear friend Iduna Stott pass out the crullers. She smiled over at her husband, who was still gloating over Corydon's ineffably ghastly versification.

"Read me some more, darling. You might as well toughen me up. There's reams of the stuff, and I suppose I'll have to plow through it all sooner or later."

Shandy was happy to oblige:

> "'Long did they seek our Gussie dear
> O'er fields and stones and stocks—
> Who knew he lay 'neath Oozak's ooze
> With his pockets full of rocks?
> Long time he lay until at last
> Augustus 'gan to bloat,
> Yet still his corse was holden fast
> By the rocks within his coat.
> Now comes release. The cloth gives way
> That causèd him to sink;
> Chewed by an otter, some folk say,
> Though perchance it was a mink.'"

"Perchance we need a drink." Helen pushed aside her papers. "Scotch or sherry, dear?"

"Scotch, since you're kind enough to suggest it. Unless you'd like me to do the honors?"

"No, sit still. My nose needs a rest from all that dust. Why don't you finish the poem and give me a brief synopsis when I come back?"

"I thought you wanted to get toughened up."

"How tough do you want me to be, for goodness' sake? Corydon does tend to go on, you know."

He did, and Shandy relished every staggering metric foot, especially when he got to the stanzas in which

Corydon proved beyond question that Augustus had not hurled himself into Oozak's Pond in a fit of depression brought on by reading the collected works of Felicia D. Hemans, as had been conjectured. He had, in fact, been stabbed in the back with a butcher knife and weighted down with two stone balls off the ornamental gateposts in front of a house until recently occupied by a mysterious stranger calling himself Henry J. Doe. Mr. Doe and Mr. Buggins had had a falling-out over the sale of a horse. It was considered significant that Mr. Doe and the horse had both vanished during that same direful night when Augustus failed for the first time in many years of happy wedlock to return to the waiting arms of his justly fearful wife. Corydon wound up with a pious postlude:

> "'May retribution follow soon
> Upon Doe's wicked heels,
> For preyful man should gain no boon
> From e'er a horse he steals.
> And may Repentance, clad in white,
> Touch heartless Henry Doe
> And may he rue both day and night
> That Gus he laid so low.'"

"Corydon really struggled over that line," said Helen returning with the drinks to hear Shandy still reading aloud. "In my opinion, he lost. Is that all, I hope?"

"We're galloping down the homestretch," Shandy reassured her. "Just listen to this:

> "'For Gus is mourned by friend and brother
> And also by his aged mother.
> Tho' waterlogged in death, may he
> Enjoy a dry eternity,
> While still we dwell with mem'ry fond
> Upon the corpse in Oozak's pond.'"

"Catchy," said Helen, "winding up with a couple of couplets. I must make a note. Do you suppose Augustus's ghost ever went sloshing around the pond afterward?"

"Oh, no question about it. I'll bet you dollars to doughnuts Corydon wrote another poem about the squelching specter."

Helen sighed. "I'm afraid you may be right. Well, let's hope Augustus doesn't take a notion to show up tomorrow. You know what a stickler Sieglinde Svenson is for the proprieties. Our dear president's wife wouldn't consider a shade who'd got his mortal coil shuffled off in a fight over a horse trade an edifying influence on the future farmers of Balaclava County."

Chapter 2

The Shandys were used to early rising; nevertheless, it took a certain amount of fortitude to haul themselves out of bed at half past five the next morning. The room was still almost dark when Shandy pulled the curtains aside.

"Flurrying a little," he reported. "That's good. Too overcast for Beauregard to see his shadow and not stormy enough to spoil the fun."

"Provided the snow doesn't make the crullers soggy." Helen was fishing her thermal underwear out of a dresser drawer. "I get to ride on the sled, you know. The bottom's going to be filled with straw for insulation, thank goodness. Iduna, Mrs. Mouzouka, and I are being picked up at the college dining room, along with the urns and baskets, so I'm afraid you'll have to find yourself another woman."

"I don't know which rite of spring you think we're expected to perform on this expedition, madam, but I assure you I shan't need any serendipitous female to perform it with," Shandy replied austerely. "I shall eat my cruller in solitary decorum, though not on an empty stomach. Mightn't it be prudent to leave here with something hot under our belts?"

"Such as what? Would a cup of tea and a piece of toast sustain you?"

"It might, if there happened to be a poached egg on top of the toast. Shall I go down and put the kettle on?"

"Do." Helen reached for a fleecy blue sweater that

matched her eyes and dragged it over her short blond curls. "Drop an egg for me, while you're about it. The poacher's in the top left-hand drawer. And be sure to butter the toast."

"Save your nagging till it's needed, woman. I was buttering toast for my oldest nephew while you were yet a babe in arms. Speaking of which—"

"Darling, not now." Somewhat reluctantly, Helen wriggled out of Peter's embrace. "Duty calls, and we must obey, or Beauregard may get huffy and refuse to cooperate. Who gets to pull him out this year, by the way?"

"John Enderble's still head man in charge of groundhog rousting."

Professor Emeritus Enderble, expert on local fauna and author of that much-lauded best-seller *How to Live with the Burrowing Mammals,* was certainly the man for the job. As the Shandys left their house, they could see John and his wife, Mary, both of them bundled up against the cold, already climbing the path that led to the campus and ultimately to the top of the hill where Oozak's Pond lay open to the flake-filled sky. Shandy dropped Helen off at the faculty dining room, then hurried to catch up with the Enderbles in case the elderly pair might need an unobtrusive helping hand up the hill.

No, they wouldn't. A group of students were swooping down, dragging a couple of handsleds bravely decked out with sheepskins, pillows, and Balaclava banners. Mary Enderble was gallantly assisted onto one and John, after a bit of coaxing, onto the other. As many young people as could get a handhold tagged on to the two ropes, while the rest swarmed around the sleds yelling "Mush! Mush!"

"We're supposed to be hollering 'Make way for the groundhog king and queen' one musher explained to Professor Shandy, "but that sounds kind of sappy, so we decided to stick with 'Mush! Mush!'"

"I'm sure Professor and Mrs. Enderble would rather have it this way," Shandy assured him.

What mattered wasn't the racket they were making but the thought behind it. He might have known the students would think of a way to spare them the cold climb. Balaclava lads and lasses were a remarkably decent lot, on the whole, and anybody who wasn't, damned soon got a little decency pounded into him by his classmates.

Shandy and the mush brigade were halfway up the hill when the great sled passed them: Odin, Thor, Hoenir, and Heimdallr in the shafts and the president himself holding the reins. Mrs. Svenson was right up there with him, naturally. Sieglinde knew better than to trust Thorkjeld Svenson out of her sight at a time like this.

Helen looked like a snowflake fairy between the statuesque Mrs. Svenson and the billowing Iduna Stott. Even Mrs. Mouzouka, head of the cookery department and no puny figure herself, was dwarfed by these two Valkyries. Iduna was blowing kisses to the cheering multitudes. Helen and Mrs. Mouzouka were smiling and waving. Sieglinde Svenson, serene and beautiful even in a blue nylon ski jacket and pants, kept raising her hand with the palm-outward gesture favored by royalty everywhere. That she happened to be wearing a fuzzy red mitten instead of a sleek white glove in no way diminished the dignity of the gesture.

Faculty folk were out in force. Shandy spied his next-door neighbors the Jackmans with their four children, all six of them togged out in identical cross-country ski suits. Dickie was washing Wendy's face with snow. Wendy was howling. Now Wendy was kicking Dickie in the shins and Dickie was howling. Shandy steered away from the Jackmans.

A good many townspeople were swelling the throng. Fred Ottermole, Balaclava Junction's police chief and almost its entire force, was there with his pretty wife, Edna

Mae, and their four sons. The Ottermole kids were less dashingly garbed than the Jackman quartet but a lot better behaved. Shandy also recognized Mrs. Betsy Lomax, who cleaned for him and Helen twice a week. She was with Mrs. Purvis Mink, wife of a college security guard. Mrs. Mink had at last got her gallstones out and appeared to be in fine fettle. So did Cronkite Swope, demon reporter for the *Balaclava County Weekly Fane and Pennon.* He was already poising his new camera to record the moment of truth for his vast reading public.

The urns were broached, the cocoa flowed. The crullers were passed around from huge flat baskets woven by students in Pam Waggoner's native arts class. Then John Enderble took his post in front of Beauregard's den, and the countdown began.

"Five, four, three, two, one—*Groundhog!*"

This was it. Professor Enderble reached into the hole, hauled out a fat bundle of gray-brown fur, and held it up for Cronkite Swope to photograph. One might have thought the roar of the crowd would already have wakened Beauregard, but it hadn't. Only after Enderble had addressed the woodchuck kindly but firmly, reminding him that the time had come to perform that once-a-year stint for which he was so well fed and housed by the college, did Beauregard consent to rouse himself.

Enderble set him down on the trodden snow. Professor Stott, hog expert nonpareil, hence official adjudicator of groundhog shadows, bent his head in earnest scrutiny, then performed a jocular thumbs-down. Even wilder cheers erupted. Enderble picked up Beauregard, thanked him for his cooperation even though he was already dozing again, and returned him to his lair as Cronkite Swope snapped yet another photograph.

Now the bonfire was alight, cracking and snapping and sending curls of fragrant blue smoke over Oozak's Pond. The seemingly bottomless cocoa urns were again in service. Reheaped baskets of crullers were being carried by willing students to those spectators too far back to get at the sled so that nobody would be left out.

Peter Shandy, a compulsive counter, tried to compute how many crullers were being masticated by how many eager mandibles this gala morning. He knew he'd never arrive at an accurate figure, but he kept counting anyway. The effort gave him an excuse to stand alone on a little mound, like Napoleon at Ratisbon, looking over the crowd.

The bonfire was blazing finely. Shandy could feel its welcome heat from where he stood. The heat was melting the ice around the pond, but that was all to the good. The pond had to be kept flowing or the methane plant wouldn't work.

Being spring fed, the Skunk Works Reservoir, as Oozak's Pond was now generally called, never froze solid, anyway. One of the first things freshmen learned was to stay off its unsafe ice in the winter. The Wash Pond, larger, more conveniently situated, and kept clear of snow, was where the students skated and the faculty curled. Except for this one day out of the school year, nobody came up here much except plant maintenance staff and security guards. Beauregard probably didn't mind being left to himself.

The snowman representing Old Man Winter was growing fast. Somebody had brought a ladder from one of the storage barns. A tall student was up on it, taking a hard-packed ball that was being passed up to him and fitting it as a head. A redheaded young woman was right behind him waving a bright headscarf, demanding that the effigy put it on and become Old Woman Winter as a blow for equal rights.

The redhead reminded Shandy a little of Birgit, the Svensons' fire-eating fifth daughter, now married to former honor student Hjalmar Olafssen and raising, as Birgit and Hjalmar would naturally do, a superior strain of raspberries. Shandy hadn't yet seen their new baby and wasn't sure he wanted to. It was said to be the spitting image of its maternal grandfather. Thus musing, he'd just accepted another cruller from a passing basket when the redhead screamed.

Of course there'd been plenty of screaming already, but this was a different kind of scream. Shandy's first thought was that the ladder was tipping over, but it wasn't. Then he realized the woman was pointing at something floating in the pond, among the melting cakes of broken ice.

Shandy had been out looking for pileated woodpeckers the day before, and he still had his field glasses in his windbreaker pocket. He whipped them out, took one quick look, and made a dash for the bank.

Somebody was yelling, "Aw, it's only a dummy." Shandy's binoculars were good ones; he knew better. He glanced at the cruller he was still holding, began to feel queasy, and dropped it unobtrusively in the slush.

Spectators were crowding forward. Chief Ottermole was trying to keep them away from the bank but not having much luck until President Svenson bulldozed his way to the fore yelling, "Stand back!"

Knowing they'd damned well better obey or he'd start picking them up two by two and hurling them into snowbanks, the mob receded. With the area safely cleared, Svenson planted himself in front of the bonfire, raised his mighty arms and bellowed, "Shut up!"

Absolute silence fell upon the throng. Even Wendy Jackman didn't dare to whimper. Then Svenson did what Shandy had feared he'd do. "Shandy," he ordered, "tell 'em."

There was no escape. Peter Shandy, by the vicissitudes of fate and the iron will of Thorkjeld Svenson, had become Balaclava's expert on bodies found in unexpected places. He cleared his throat and raised his voice.

"It looks as if there's been a drowning. I don't know who.

You can forget about rescue; the victim is far beyond help."

He held up his field glasses to show them how he knew. "Our maintenance crew has equipment to cope with the situation, and we'll get right to it. If you're ghoulish enough to stand around and watch, kindly keep out from underfoot. If you know of any local person who's been missing from home, tell Chief Ottermole now. Otherwise, you can help us most by dispersing quietly. I don't have to remind faculty and students that classes will begin at the usual time. Those due at the animal barns," he added after a signal from Professor Stott, "had better make tracks. You're half a minute late already."

Tardiness in tending the livestock was the ultimate Thou Shalt Not at Balaclava Agricultural College. Several students gasped and sprinted for the barns. They started a mass exodus. Muttering of jobs, chores, or getting the kids on the school bus, townsfolk straggled off across the campus or up the back road. A few paused to speak with Fred Ottermole, who was having his picture taken by Cronkite Swope while Edna Mae and the boys stood by basking in reflected glory.

Shandy didn't bother asking Ottermole what the informants were saying. He was dispatching students to fetch the rubber dinghy kept at the methane plant for working on the sluices, to bring one of the nets used to trap floating debris and a tarpaulin to cover the body when they brought it ashore. He delegated one to call Dr. Melchett, the college physician, and another to get hold of Harry Goulson, the local mortician. Melchett would balk at a waterlogged cadaver cluttering up his swank office, but Goulson was used to taking them any way they came. Shandy only hoped to God this one wouldn't fall to pieces when they lifted it out of the water.

In less than a minute, the dinghy was brought, the oars and net put on board, and they were ready to cast off.

President Svenson moved to step aboard, but his wife hauled him back.

"Thorkjeld, you will not set foot in that little boat. You would get wet and catch a sniffle. Let Peter go."

"Why should Shandy catch a sniffle instead of me?"

"Peter will not catch a sniffle because he will not wallow around like a whale in a bathtub and sink the boat. Come now, you must drive back the sled. Mrs. Mouzouka needs the urns to make coffee for breakfast."

Rather than trust any hand but his own to drive the Balaclava Blacks in a four-horse hitch, Svenson had to obey with what grace he could muster. That would not have been much at the best of times, and this was surely one of the worse.

"Report to me later in my office, Shandy," he growled to show his was still the hand on the helm regardless of who got to ride in the boat. Then he followed his wife back to the sled.

"That's a relief," grunted Chief Ottermole, who'd been secretly terrified of losing face in front of his family. Honor demanded that he himself be among the crew, but with that behemoth aboard, there'd have been no room for a man Ottermole's size, or anybody's size. He and Shandy would fit together all right. Besides, the chief had no idea how to go about recovering the body, but it looked as if Shandy might.

Helen was none too happy at watching Shandy get stuck with the dirty work again, but there wasn't a thing she could do except bite her tongue and hope that flimsy apology for a boat would hold together. Shandy wasn't thinking much about the dinghy or anything else except what he'd seen bobbing around out there. He stepped in and settled himself between the oarlocks, feeling the boat's thin plastic bottom every whit as cold on his backside as he'd expected it to be. He held up a steadying hand to Ottermole and took the oars, the net, and the rope he'd forgotten to ask for from the student who'd been smart enough to bring it anyway. He fitted the oars into the oarlocks and handed the net and rope to the chief.

"Here, your lap's bigger than mine. I'll row. You navigate."

Ottermole was doing his manful best not to look green around the gills. "Okay, if that's the way you want it. Cripes, my ass is frozen already."

"Don't start bitching yet," Shandy warned him. "Swope's taking your picture."

Being the smaller and the older of the two, Shandy could have let the chief row; but he was a powerful man for his size and well aware that he stood less chance of a dunking if he handled the oars himself. Anyway, there wasn't much to do. A dozen good heaves on the oars brought them close enough to the body for Ottermole to abandon all pretense of having his stomach under control.

"Jeez, why'd I eat them five crullers?" he moaned as he got his first real look. Where the face should have been, there was only a grayish mist.

"Any idea who it might be?" Shandy asked him.

"Hell, no. How could you tell?"

"What about the people who were reported missing?"

"Three high school kids hitchhikin' to Boston an' old man Hooker off on another toot. This here was a middle-aged man, I'd say as a guess. Good-sized an' well fed, though that might just be the body blowin' up from—" The chief paused to deal with some poignant inner conflict.

Peter Shandy was a man of the turnip fields. Furthermore, he'd refrained from eating that other cruller. "Well, let's get the net around him. Flip it over the body, then we'll turn him over and wrap the other end around."

"Yeah, sure."

Ottermole gulped a mighty gulp, glanced shoreward to see whether Cronkite Swope was still taking pictures, took heart when he spied the camera pointed in his direction, and laid hold of the net.

Shandy's plan proved easier in theory than in fact, but by bringing the dinghy parallel to the corpse and each taking a corner of the net, they managed to get the body covered. Then came the grisly task of turning it over. This, they persuaded themselves, could be done better with the oars than by hand. After too much splashing and fumbling, they succeeded after a fashion, passed a bight of the rope around their dreadful catch, and towed it back to where the bonfire had melted out a viable landing place.

By now, nobody was left on the bank except Cronkite Swope. The helpful students had gone off, no doubt reluctantly, to their classes. Mrs. Ottermole had taken the boys to school. Dr. Melchett still hadn't arrived.

Melchett wasn't cut out for this kind of doctoring, Shandy thought. He'd have been happier in a Back Bay office, treating wealthy Boston ladies for nervous prostration brought on by too many charity balls. Only a perverse fate in the guise of a lucrative family practice had kept him in Balaclava Junction.

Melchetts had been the official college physicians ever since Balaclava Buggins's first student had come down with a quinsy sore throat. As the college had grown, so had the prestige of the position. Shandy wondered whether it had been the current Melchett's grandfather or his great-grandfather who'd examined the corpse Corydon Buggins had written his god-awful poem about. The god-awfulness had taken on a different tinge for him now. He knelt in the slush to unwind the net.

"Who is it?" Cronkite Swope had his notebook out. "Have you been able to identify him, Fred?"

"Not yet." Ottermole was trying not to look at the thing they'd brought back. "He's mildewed or something."

"Actually," said Shandy, "I think it's a beard. Would either of you happen to have a pocket comb?"

"You're goin' to comb his face?" gasped Ottermole.

"Unless you'd rather do it yourself."

Ottermole fumbled at one of the many zippered pockets in his black leather jacket and fished out a dainty pink plastic comb. "No, you can," he said through clenched teeth. "I got to go see if the doctor's coming."

He disappeared through a stand of spruce trees, and nobody was tactless enough to follow him. Shandy finished disentangling the appalling object from the net with some assistance from Cronkite Swope, who kept muttering to himself that Dan Rather wouldn't shirk such an assignment.

"Neither would Harry Goulson," snapped Shandy, who was none too happy about it, either.

"At least Harry could collect from the relatives," Swope argued back.

"Assuming we ever find out who the relatives are."

Shandy had to admit there was something particularly sickening about all that gray hair plastered over the dead face. Swope straightened up and focused his camera but seemed to feel it wasn't quite the thing to take a picture of the eminent Professor Shandy combing a cadaver. Then he discovered he was out of film, or said he was, and stepped back a good deal farther to reload.

Shandy was having his problems with the beard. It had picked up a considerable amount of duckweed during its immersion and was now beginning to freeze in the colder air. He did manage to sort out the whiskers from the eyebrows, which were not quite luxuriant enough to hide half-open eyes of an appropriate watery blue. He also located a nose that must have started out to become a real Yankee eagle beak and got broken somewhere along the way.

The mouth defeated him; it was hopelessly buried under all those weeds and whiskers. He'd leave that for Harry Goulson to exhume under more favorable conditions. Shandy had better luck with an ear, a large one that stuck out from the skull with force and determination and had the oversized lobe supposed to prognosticate a long and vigorous life. So much for prognostication.

Ottermole had found his man. He came striding over the rise with his uniform cap at a purposeful angle and Dr. Melchett in tow. The doctor, as Shandy had anticipated, was not happy.

"Who is it this time?"

"Don't ask me," said Shandy. "I have a feeling I've met him somewhere, but I can't seem to place him."

Melchett scrutinized the remains with professional detachment. "He does look vaguely familiar, but he's no patient of mine. Ottermole, you should know him if anyone does."

"Well, I don't. What I want to know is, how come he's wearing those funny clothes?"

"What funny clothes?" Melchett took a closer look at the sodden garments. "Why, bless my soul, so they are. Shandy, what do you make of this?"

"I don't know what to make of it. I know we New Englanders tend to hang on to things, but this outfit must be a hundred years old. Great Scott, I wonder—" On a hideous impulse, Shandy knelt beside the body and ran his hands into the clammy pockets of the tight-waisted black frock coat. He wasn't really much surprised to find they each contained one large, smooth rock.

Chapter 3

"Though perchance it was a mink," Shandy murmured, wiping his half-frozen hands on the sides of his trousers.

Cronkite Swope had quick ears. "You okay, Professor?" he asked anxiously.

"Yes, I think so. Drat, I wish Mrs. Lomax were still here."

"Aunt Betsy? What for?"

"She'd know whether there are any Bugginses still living around these parts."

"By George, yes," cried Melchett. "No wonder he looked familiar. This man's the spitting image of that daguerreotype enlargement of Balaclava Buggins you've got hanging in the foyer of the administration building. And wasn't there a suit of his kicking around somewhere? Could this be it?"

Shandy shook his head. "Not in a million years. Balaclava's Sunday go-to-meetings are preserved as a sacred relic in a glass case at the library. What's left of them, anyway. The moths got into his coattails along about 1905, my wife estimates, and nobody noticed till they'd done several decades' worth of damage."

He straightened out the coat as best he could and scrutinized the cloth. "These duds look to me to be in excellent condition, all things considered. It's my guess they may have come from a theatrical costumer or somewhere like that. Unless our stranger here had them

20

made to order, in which case he must have been well heeled enough to indulge such a whim and crazy enough to carry it through. You've lived in Balaclava Junction all your life, Melchett. Can't you think of any Buggins who might fill the bill?"

The doctor started to shake his head, then stopped. "Bracebridge! By thunder, I'll bet this is Bracebridge Buggins. Well, well, after all these years."

"How many years?" Shandy demanded.

Melchett rubbed his chin. "Let's see, would it have been in the fifties? No, earlier than that. Right after the war, say 1946 or thereabouts. Brace showed up in a rear admiral's uniform with a chestful of ribbons and a headful of yarns. He swanked around town for a few days, then disappeared, and that's the last I ever saw of him. A week or so later, a couple of men in business suits came looking for him. We never did find out who they were or what they wanted him for."

"Interesting," said Shandy. "Did he claim the broken nose was a war injury?"

"No, he didn't have it then. I wonder when it happened." Melchett made a cautious exploration. "Sometime during the past thirty years or so is the best I can do. It's not a recent break."

"Um. Grew up around here, did he?"

"Out at the Seven Forks. I never knew him well. Brace was much older than I, of course."

The hell he was, assuming this was, in fact, Bracebridge Buggins. "Getting back to my original question, are there any Bugginses living around here now?"

Melchett stared at him. "Certainly. Your neighbor Grace Porble is a direct descendant of Balaclava himself. Didn't you know that?"

Shandy had not known that. Helen did, maybe, but she'd never happened to mention it. To him, Grace Porble had always been the librarian's wife and a prominent member of the garden club, which he was occasionally asked to address. He saw a lot more of her now that she and his own wife had become friends, but he still had reservations about a woman more interested in arranging flowers than in growing them.

Grace's natural dignity of manner had led Shandy to assume she'd come from what his mother would have called a good family, but she'd never talked about her connections and Shandy was never curious enough to ask.

"Has Grace any brothers?"

"Two. Trowbridge is a geologist out west somewhere, and Boatwright's captain of a tramp steamer. Sails all over the world, they say. What a life, eh?"

"Does he ever sail back to Balaclava Junction?"

"What would he want to do that for?" Melchett replied somewhat bitterly. "No, Grace and her brothers have never been what you'd call close. Their mother died young and the father remarried."

"Is he still living?"

"No, though I believe the stepmother is. She married again, too, a real-estate broker from Florida. Anyway, the boys resented her and took off as soon as they could. Grace got along with her all right, as far as I know. Grace was the youngest by several years, so I suppose she adjusted more easily. Anyway, she stayed home and went to Simmons. I think she hoped to become the college librarian, but while she was still an undergratuate, old Dr. Brinkle died and Phil Porble was hired to replace him. The upshot was that Grace and Phil were married right after her graduation. A very suitable match, my wife and I have always felt," Dr. Melchett added rather pompously, "though it wasn't an impressive wedding. Grace's cousin was her only atten- dant."

"Was this a Buggins cousin?" Shandy asked him.

"Yes, Persephone, that was. Bracebridge's sister, come to

think of it. She's Mrs. Mink now. Her husband's one of your security guards."

"Mrs. Purvis Mink, then. The one with the gallstones. Or without them, I should say."

"Quite right," said Melchett crisply, somewhat put out by Shandy's touch of levity. "Sephy never had Grace's advantages, needless to say."

"Purvis Mink's a damned good man," barked Chief Ottermole, equally nettled by Melchett's intimation that any law-enforcement officer could be in any way inferior to a pantywaist librarian.

"I'm not saying he isn't," Melchett snapped back. "However, the simple fact of the matter is that Persephone came from Ichabod's stock instead of Balaclava's. You know as well as I do that none of the Ichabod Buggins line ever amounted to a row of pins."

"Oh yeah? Then how about Bracebridge gettin' to be a rear admiral?"

"How about those two men who came looking for him? Putting on a uniform doesn't necessarily mean you're entitled to wear it."

"M'yes," said Shandy. "You have a point there, Melchett. If this is in fact Bracebridge Buggins, perhaps these odd clothes he has on could be merely another expression of a penchant for fancy dress. Were he and Persephone the only siblings?"

"No. Brace had a twin bother, Bainbridge. Bain ran away and joined the army while he was still in high school. There was a bit of a stink because he lied about his age and forged his father's name on the papers. The parents were upset, but not enough to go to the authorities and get him released before he was sent overseas into combat. Those twins had been nothing but trouble since the day they were born. Anyway, Bainbridge never came back."

"Do you mean he was killed in action?"

"That was the general assumption. I can't tell you for

sure. I was away at prep school then myself. You wouldn't remember, Ottermole?"

"Hell, no. I wasn't even born."

One up for the boys in blue. Shandy might have been amused if his mind weren't still on the Bugginses. "What were the parents' names? Is either of them still living?"

"I think they both are," said Melchett. "Trevelyan and Beatrice were still hanging on at the old Ichabod Buggins homestead last I saw of them, though neither is in good health."

"Purve's Aunt Minerva lives with 'em," Ottermole interjected. "They'd have tough sledding without old Min to keep things going."

"Yes, Miss Mink's a grand old gal," Melchett replied automatically, that being the accepted cliché for elderly women still in possession of their faculties. "Well, I can't do anything more here, and I'm due for my hospital rounds. Death by drowning, on the face of it."

"How long was the body in the water?" Shandy asked him, not expecting a firm answer and not getting one.

"That's a bit tricky, considering the water temperature and so forth. Not a great while, I shouldn't think, maybe a week or two. I'd really prefer you get on to the county medical examiner."

As the doctor bustled away, Ottermole snorted. "Trust Melchett to pass the buck. Anyhow, we accomplished something. I better get hold of Sephy Mink. She'd be the best one to make an indentification, huh?"

"She or her parents," Shandy agreed, "unless they're too rocky. If I were you, though, I'd let Goulson, er, tidy him up first. I couldn't make much headway with that beard. I'm afraid I broke some teeth out of your comb trying to pry the duckweed loose."

"That's okay. I can't say I'd feel much like using it again, anyway."

Ottermole flipped the shard of pink plastic into the

pond. He, Shandy, and Swope had been to the well together,* he didn't have to be indomitable in front of them. "What the heck's keeping Harry, anyway?"

"I'll run down and phone him, if you like," offered Cronkite Swope. "I ought to get hold of my editor, too, and tell him there's a big story breaking."

"Yeah, tell 'em to tear out the front page," said Otter-mole.

"They won't have set it yet," Swope reassured him. "Does the Skunk Works have a phone I can call from, Professor?"

"No, just an intercom. You'll have to use the pay phone in the administration building. Here's some change if you need it."

Telephones were one of President Svenson's economies. Professors were paid to teach students, not chin with outsiders. Students were to listen and learn. Staff members were paid to work. The fewer phones available, the less apt everybody would be to waste time in idle chitchat and run up the overhead.

Nobody would have disputed Thorkjeld Svenson's logic even if they'd had the guts to try. Everyone knew the savings from his many penny-pinchings filtered back in better pay for staff and faculty, better food, better student housing, and an absence of the leaping tuition rates that afflicted less tautly run institutions. Well aware of Bala-clava's fiscal policies, Cronkite Swope accepted Shandy's change and galloped phoneward.

As it happened, Swope saved Shandy a quarter. Harry Goulson passed him on the way, jockeying a van painted a discreet charcoal-gray with a chaste white dove carrying a laurel wreath in its beak across the front panel. The reporter wavered. Should he rush back up the hill and take a picture of the undertaker emerging from his van?

*Something the Cat Dragged In, 1983.

Should he press on and call his editor, who must by now be foaming at the mouth because Cronk hadn't yet shown up with a whimsical tidbit about Balaclava Beauregard? Little did the editor know.

Fortified by his knowledge of what his chief didn't know and aware that Harry Goulson wasn't one to rush, since his customers never got up and walked out on him, Swope kept going. It was as well he did. Goulson's van got stuck in the slush. The undertaker and Fred Ottermole had to put their backs to the bumper and shove, while Peter Shandy tried all the different gears and finally hit on one that worked.

Once the van was back on terra more or less firma, they decided they'd better leave it there and bring the corpse down to it. By the time Swope got back, he found the remains neatly disposed on a stretcher, rigor having passed off who knew how long ago, and Harry Goulson bent over it, pondering.

"Were Bracebridge and Bainbridge identical twins?" Professor Shandy was asking.

"They were and they weren't" was Goulson's unsatisfactory reply. "What I mean is, you could tell them apart when they were together, but it was tough when they were apart. Added to which, I haven't laid eyes on either one of them for maybe forty years."

"So you can't say for sure whether this is Bracebridge or Bainbridge?"

"To be honest with you, I wouldn't want to swear it's either one of them. He was a Buggins, I'd be willing to bet my last jug of formaldehyde on that. He ought to be Brace, because Bain was reported missing right after the Normandy invasion, in 1944. Offhand, I can't think who else he could be. There's a few what you might call unofficial Bugginses around Balaclava County, Belial having been the kind of man he was, which I don't have to tell you because you know Henny Horsefall's Aunt Hilda. But that was a long time ago, and they've sort of petered out. Sorry, Professor, I didn't mean to take your name in vain."

"I'm used to it," Shandy reassured him. "Whoever he is, we might as well get him into the van. Ottermole wants to bring Persephone Mink over to your place, hoping she'll be able to make a positive identification. If she can't, we'll have to ask the parents."

"Now that," said Goulson, "is what you can't do. See, they're the reason I was so late getting here."

"Great balls of fire! You don't mean to tell me they're dead, too?"

"Yup. Got 'em both tucked away side by side in the cold room right now. You know, that was a queer thing. Maybe not so queer, you'd say, considering they were both in their eighties and pretty shaky on their pins. Still and all, you know how it is with the creaking gates, as we call 'em in the trade. My own professional estimate would have been that old Trevelyan ought to have hit ninety and Beatrice might have outlasted him a year or two. But be cussed and be blowed if they didn't pass to their rewards last night."

"Both at the same time?" demanded Fred Ottermole.

"'Fraid I can't answer that one, Fred. All I know is, Miss Mink went to take them their breakfast this morning about ten to six, just as I was getting my boots on to come up here and see what Beauregard had to report, as a matter of fact, the boy being off to embalming school as you know and Mrs. Goulson not being keen to get rousted out that early. She was out late last night covering the installation at the Ladies of the Sunbeam."

"Arabella does the society news for the *Fane and Pennon*," Cronkite Swope put in, as if anyone had to be told.

"That's right," said Goulson. "Arabella knew you'd be here for the big event, Cronk, and doing a fine job as usual. But anyway, Miss Mink went upstairs to the bedroom, as I said, and there they were. Stiff and stark in their flannelette nightgowns, united in their passing as in their lives. And Miss Mink stuck with two extra plates of porridge and nobody to eat 'em."

"She could do like Edna Mae does," Chief Ottermole suggested. "Fry it like pancakes an' pour maple syrup over it. Ugh! I wish I hadn't said that. Both of 'em in one night? Cripes, that's something."

It was something, all right. Shandy wanted a more precise definition. "Did Miss Mink call the doctor? Melchett didn't say anything about that."

"She called me first," said Goulson. "I said I'd go right out, which I did, but in the meantime she should call Dr. Fotheringay. They were his patients, not Melchett's. We got there just about the same time."

"And did Dr. Fotheringay sign death certificates before you took the bodies away?"

"Yup. Both loved ones laid to rest with one stroke of the pen, as you might say. Actually, the doctor's ballpoint wasn't working too good, so Miss Mink had to go and hunt him up one of those big fat brown ones shaped like a wienie that Sam's Hot Doggery was giving out last summer with their Gourmet Special. Miss Mink was kind of upset over the doctor's having to use such an undignified pen for so solemn an occasion. As I told her, though, I don't suppose Saint Peter's going to hold a little thing like that against Beatrice and Trevelyan when they get to the pearly gates."

"You have a genius for the *mot juste,* Goulson," said Shandy. "What did Fotheringay put down as the cause of death, do you recall?"

"Let's see now. Beatrice was pulmonary failure, and Trev was cardiac arrest. Or was it the other way around? I'm so bollixed up, what with three demises in a row before I've even had time to get a hot breakfast into me, that I hardly know which end I'm standing on. Miss Mink did offer me a plate of porridge, but somehow I couldn't warm up to it."

Shandy cleared his throat. "Cardiac arrest and pulmonary failure, eh? That's rather a portmanteau kind of diagnosis, isn't it?"

"It's what Doc Fotheringay generally puts for people their age. One or the other, I mean. Only this time he got to use both."

"I see. But did he perform a thorough examination before he arrived at his conclusions?"

"I wouldn't know about that, Professor. Professional etiquette demanded that I stand back and let the doctor go first, so I waited downstairs. That was when Miss Mink offered me the porridge. And then he came down and handed me the forms and said he was going home to get his breakfast. As was right and proper."

"I'm sure it was," said Shandy. "Nevertheless, Ottermole, I expect you're thinking that since the circumstances are so, er, unusual, you're planning to instruct the medical examiner to take a look at the elder Bugginses, along with our chap here, before Goulson goes ahead with the proceedings."

"Yeah, sure," Ottermole lied bravely. "You took the words right out of my mouth, Professor. I bet you even know what I'm going to do next," he added, being not without guile.

"Well, I'd suppose you're planning to drop over for a chat with Miss Mink," Shandy obliged him by saying. "If you need someone to take notes, I'd be glad to ride along with you."

"Why not? The more the merrier. Cronk can come, too, and take pictures. We might as well stop an' pick up Sephy Mink while we're about it, unless she's there already."

"Drat," said Shandy. "She was right here a while back. I saw her with Mrs. Lomax."

"Yeah," snarled the chief, "an' maybe she'd still be here if you hadn't given everybody the bum's rush an' made 'em miss watching me bring in the body. Want me to go get the police cruiser? She's popped her last spring, an' I'm none too sure about the master cylinder, but she might hold together long enough to take us there."

The professor knew Ottermole was hinting to use the Shandy car and didn't blame him a whit. He was about to offer when Cronkite Swope beat him to it.

"We can ride in the press car if you want, Fred."

"Huh? I didn't know there was one."

"Heck, yes. The *Fane and Pennon* moves with the times. After I took that header off my motorcycle and landed in the hospital, Mr. Droggins, the editor, went straight over to Lunatic Louie's used-car lot and bought a 1974 Plymouth Valiant."

"Decent of him," Shandy grunted.

Considering how much Swope had done to boost the *Fane and Pennon's* circulation to its present dizzy height and how close he'd come to killing himself in the line of duty, Shandy didn't see why Droggins couldn't have sprung for a later model. But he didn't say so. He was thinking about those two old people and the porridge they'd never got to eat and about those two smooth rocks in the old frock coat and the duckweed freezing in a dead man's beard.

The others must have been thinking much the same as he. Nobody spoke a word as Goulson and Ottermole picked up the stretcher and slid it into the van. Only the faint clicking of Cronkite Swope's camera shutter disturbed the eerie calm that had fallen over Oozak's Pond.

Chapter 4

"**M**y God, what's that?"

Well might Chief Ottermole ask. From below the hill, shattering the stillness, came a roaring and a rattling, a wild tintinnabulation of bells and a Plutonian thunder of hooves.

"It's either Lützow's Wild Hunt or President Svenson out for another little spin with the Blacks," Shandy guessed, and the latter it proved to be.

Svenson was standing up in the sled, leaning forward like Ben Hur on the last lap. His gray knitted cap was gone with the wind, his gray-black hair in tumultuous disarray. He was slapping his reins, urging the Blacks to breakneck speed, and the howls that emerged from his cavernous throat sounded all too dreadfully like "Shandy! Shandy! Shandy!"

Peter Shandy stepped well clear of the path and waved his arms, knowing he couldn't possibly make himself heard above the hullabaloo. Catching his signal, Svenson somehow brought the equine typhoon to a safe halt. Shandy walked over to the smoking beasts, of whom the one holding the reins was surely the smokiest.

"Practicing up for the Charge of the Light Brigade, President?" he asked sociably.

"Arrgh! We got a letter."

"We? You mean you and Sieglinde or you and I?"

"I mean the college, damn it. Get in."

One did not argue with Thorkjeld Svenson on petty

questions of life and limb. Shandy merely suggested to
Ottermole and Swope that they pick up Mrs. Mink and
wait for him at Goulson's, then he got.

"Do I gather you wish me to read this letter, President?"

"Urrgh!"

Svenson thrust the paper into his hands and turned the
Blacks, without yanking on the reins. Enraged though he
might be, indeed as he often was, Balaclava's president had
never been known to treat a child or an animal with
anything other than fatherly kindness. Shandy settled
himself among the straw that still half filled the sled and
began to read. Halfway through the letter, he exploded.

"Good God, President, this is outrageous!"

"Arrgh," Svenson agreed.

"They must be stark, raving lunatics."

"Ungh."

"It says here that the college doesn't own Oozak's Pond."

"I know what it says," Svenson bellowed. "What are you
going to do about it?"

"Me?"

"What the hell do you think we pay you for?"

"Well, er, I've always assumed it was for teaching
agronomy."

Svenson emitted a snort.

"Does that mean I'm relieved from my classes?"

"No. Who the hell was Ichabod Buggins?"

"M'well, I shouldn't be overwhelmingly surprised to
learn he was the great-grandfather of the man we just
found in the pond dressed up as Augustus."

"Augustus who?"

"Buggins, naturally. He was Balaclava's grandson."

"Talk sense."

Shandy talked what sense he could, which was not a
great deal once he got into the Bracebridge-Bainbridge
area. The cloud over Svenson's brow grew blacker than the

coat on Loki's back. He flipped the reins and turned the sled again.

"Where in tunket are you headed now?" Shandy demanded.

"Goulson's. Drop you off."

"I can walk, thanks."

"Blah."

Shandy resigned himself and went back to the disturbing missive. The gist of it was that attorneys Patter, Potter, Patter, and Foote had been retained by heirs of the late Ichabod Buggins to defend their rights with regard to a certain parcel of land described in tedious detail but boiling down to the acre containing the body of water known since 1765 and so depicted on early town maps as Oozak's Pond.

The college was alleged to have been committing acts of trespass and illegally diverting water out of the pond for its own purposes ever since its founding, at which time Oozak's Pond was already owned by Ichabod Buggins.

Unless an agreement could be reached on the amount of reparations due, retroactive to the date when the first college cow took its first bootleg swig from the pond—the legal phraseology was obfuscated, but Shandy caught its meaning easily enough—the water supply would be summarily cut off. This meant that the college and other properties served by the methane plant—Shandy's own house among them—would be without power until another source could be provided.

"This is utter hogwash," Shandy snorted. "Balaclava Buggins owned the pond and all the land around it."

"Says he didn't."

"I know what it says. They're claiming Balaclava gambled the pond away to Ichabod's father, Abelard, in a sporting wager, whatever that's supposed to mean. When did Balaclava Buggins ever gamble?"

"Gambled on starting the college."

"That was no gamble. It was a calculated risk based on a sound premise. Anyway, if Balaclava did indulge in an occasional spree of horseshoe pitching or whatever, he'd have known better than to bet on the outcome with that horse-trading brother of his."

"Might have been drunk."

"M'yes, that's always a possibility." After all, their founder had invented the Balaclava Boomerang, a combination of homemade cherry brandy and home-hardened cider that was hardly a tipple for the timid tippler. "But Abelard would have been drunker," Shandy insisted. "He was a two-fisted toper."

"Stayed sober long enough to con Oozak's Pond out of old Balaclava."

"Abelard Buggins did nothing of the sort. Nor did his alleged heir, Ichabod." Shandy didn't often raise his voice in anger, but he was raising it now.

Svenson saw him and raised him. "How the hell do you know?"

"By the twitching of my thumbs."

"Try taking a twitch into a courtroom. They say they've got proof."

"To quote you, blah! I'll believe their proof when I see it, provided it hasn't been faked, which you can bet your boots it has. The Bugginses were always fantastic practical jokers, you know that as well as I do. Look, President, you don't need me to get you out of this one. You need Helen and a lawyer."

"Helen's your wife."

"So what? Helen is a distinguished scholar, an authority on the Buggins family, and a member of the college in her own right."

"Urrgh!"

Svenson's final argument was irrefutable. Anyway, they were coming to Harry Goulson's big white clapboard house now, the sled runners grating hideously over the bare spots on Main Street. The president brought his team to a halt, apparently by thought transference, and Shandy climbed down.

A banged-up green Valiant with a press card stuck behind the windshield was sitting out front. His cohorts had arrived. In fact, they were already coming back out. Persephone Mink was walking a step ahead of Ottermole and Swope. She looked both forlorn and mulish.

"He could o' been wearin' blue contact lenses," Fred Ottermole was arguing.

"Blue contact lenses, my eyeball," sniffed Persephone. "D' you think I wouldn't know my own brothuh?"

"But you ain't seen neither Brace nor Bain since you was a kid."

Mrs. Mink didn't answer, merely buttoned her decent black coat up under her chin and gave a smart tug to the black scarf with red spots she'd tied over her hair. Time was when any Balaclava County matron would have kept a black hat in her closet for occasions such as this or at least had an aunt handy she could borrow one from. Things were different nowadays. Shandy was rather surprised Sephy had bothered about mourning clothes at all. To be sure, the red polka dots were a bit frisky, but at least the black scarf showed she'd done the best she could with what she had.

Maybe Purve had reminded her about the proprieties. Purvis Mink was a bit of a stickler, as any security guard who expected to get along with joint chiefs of staff Clarence and Silvester Lomax would have to be. Perhaps Persephone was a stickler herself. Mrs. Lomax thought a lot of Sephy Mink, Shandy knew. She'd said so often enough. He took off his aged tweed hat.

"Good morning, Mrs. Mink. I'm sorry to hear of your bereavement."

"Thank you, Professuh. I'm none too pleased about it myself, though I'm not quite so bereft as Fred heah seems to think," she replied, snipping off her *r*'s like a true Balaclava County native. They wouldn't go to waste; she'd use them up in words like *sawring* and *drawring* and *idear*. "'Scuse me, I'm on my way to the pahsonage."

Persephone went. Ottermole stayed put, shaking his head. "She claims it ain't neither one of the twins."

"What was that you said about contact lenses?" Shandy asked him.

"She claims Brace an' Bain both had brown eyes. This here stiff's eyes are blue, so that's how she knows he ain't them."

"Drat. Unless the man did in fact happen to be wearing tinted lenses. Did you ask Goulson?"

"Never thought of it myself till just this minute," the police chief admitted.

"Then let's go back and ask him now."

Shandy led the way through the Goulsons' tastefully decorated hallway, careful to step only on the transparent plastic runners Arabella had laid down over the gray plush carpeting, and on to Goulson's workroom. The undertaker wasn't working now, merely standing there with a melancholy expression on his wontedly genial face.

"Hello, Professor. Looks as if we struck out."

"So Ottermole was just telling me. Would he by any chance have tinted contact lenses?"

"Nope. I thought of them myself right off the bat when she said the boys' eyes were brown."

"And were they?"

Goulson hunched his shoulders. "Their own sister ought to know. I guess maybe they were—sort of hazely brown. So that means we're back where we started, eh?"

"I expect something will turn up once the word gets around," said Shandy. If he knew this town, the news was well on its way already. "Did the medical examiner tell you when he'd be over, Ottermole?"

"He said he'd make it as quick as he could."

Ottermole grinned. "He says he always enjoys comin' here because we get the most int'restin' corpses."

"Ungh," said Shandy, since Thorkjeld Svenson wasn't here to say it for him. "I'm glad somebody gets a kick out of our misfortunes. You might as well get on with watering the potted palms or whatever's on your agenda, Goulson. You, er, won't want to touch any of the bodies until the medical examiner has seen them, I'm sure. We'll check back with you in a while. Come along, Swope. Save your film for Miss Mink."

"We still going to see her?" Chief Ottermole asked in some surprise.

"Why not?" said Shandy. "Trevelyan Buggins and his wife are still dead, aren't they?"

"Were the last time I looked at 'em," said Harry Goulson with a return of his customary joviality. "Sephy Mink asked to view the remains, as was only natural, them being her parents. I gave it as my professional opinion that the passing of the loved ones was a blessed release, and she agreed."

"She didn't say who was gettin' released, I noticed," Ottermole grunted. "I guess it won't break her an' Purve's hearts not to be runnin' out to First Fork three or four times a week, fetchin' and carryin' an' helpin' out with the chores, which usually meant doin' it all themselves."

"Well, now, that's something I wouldn't be too sure of myself," said the undertaker. "Time and again I've noticed it's the ones people do the most for who they miss the worst. Persephone Mink's not a person to give way in public, no more than you or I, but she's feeling her loss."

He nodded, more to himself than to his hearers. "Yes, she's feeling it, poor soul. And she'll feel it a darned sight harder once she's had time to sit down and think about it. Maybe I ought to give Betsy Lomax a ring so she can slip over to the Minks' and have a cup of hot tea waiting for Sephy when she gets back from talking to the minister.

Knowing Betsy, though, I shouldn't be surprised if she's already there with the kettle on the simmer. Purve's gone to work, I suppose?"

"He went," said Ottermole. "I don't know if he stayed. Purve's on the day shift this week. Cronk and I met him on the road. He was runnin' late. He told us his aunt had called to give 'em the word after Sephy left for the doin's up at the pond, and he'd waited till she came back so he could break it to her easy. He didn't much like leavin' her, but he said he figured he'd better at least check in at the security office an' hang around till Clarence an' Sil could find somebody to cover for him."

"I suppose it's hard to know where your priorities are at a time like this," said Cronkite Swope, who'd been remarkably silent up to now, for him.

"Yeah, 'specially with President Svenson breathin' fire down your neck if he thinks you're slackin' your job."

"President Svenson would work the shift himself, if he had to, rather than put pressure on a man with a family crisis on his hands," Shandy retorted somewhat stiffly.

Then again, if Thorkjeld Svenson had known Purve's wife was not only a Buggins but a descendant of the accursed Ichabod—and he might, because the president always knew what you least wanted him to—he might have taken the alternative course of tearing Purve limb from limb and stamping on the pieces. Maybe it was as well Mink had elected to show up at the office.

Shandy told Goulson again that he'd see him later and followed Swope and Ottermole out to the green Valiant. Cronkite Swope was no slouch at the wheel, he soon found; nevertheless, the ride out to First Fork seemed a dull and pallid affair after the Nantucket sleighride with Svenson and the Blacks.

The Ichabod Buggins homestead was a dull and pallid affair, too. It couldn't be called ramshackle, exactly. Purvis and Persephone Mink had obviously done what they could. Plastic storm windows had been tacked over the dried-out wooden sashes. Trash hadn't been allowed to collect in the dooryard beyond a reasonable limit. Paint had been applied to the withered clapboards, possibly within the present decade.

But Purve and Sephy had their own place to keep up, and there was just so much one could do to a house that had been sliding downhill for a century or more, short of tearing it down and starting over. Ichabod couldn't have left his heirs much to go on with, and those who followed him wouldn't have done enough better to make much of a difference.

Shandy knew all about the Ichabods, the families that barely managed to scrape along from generation to generation. It was generally the weaker vessels that hung around the old place. They'd have an ill-tended plot out back where they'd raise some garden sass in the summertime, if their few stringy hens didn't scratch up all the seed before the plants got going. Maybe there'd be a pig in a makeshift pen when they could raise the price of a shoat and scrounge enough garbage to fatten it on. They'd hunt and fish and do odd jobs now and then and get by somehow.

Those with any gumption either pitched in and turned the family fortunes around, which clearly hadn't happened here, or got out and made lives for themselves somewhere else. If they happened to find their niche nearby, like Sephy, they'd drop over and lend a hand when they got the chance. If they moved far away, they'd maybe send a money order now and then. Bainbridge mightn't have lived long enough to do much in that way.

Then there were the ones who just cleared out and tried to forget where they'd come from. Bracebridge Buggins sounded like one of those, from the way Dr. Melchett had described him. But how far had he gotten?

He hadn't landed in Oozak's Pond, anyway, unless his

sister was lying and Harry Goulson was backing her up.
What in Sam Hill would they do that for? Unless Persephone Mink happened to be the one who'd instigated
this mad lawsuit against the college and Harry was hoping
for some hush money out of the proceeds.

Shandy could not see Harry Goulson lending his good
name to any such shenanigans. Aside from the ethical
question of would he, there was the practical one of why
the hell should he?

Goulson had been born to affluence, by Balaclava
Junction standards. When his father passed on, Goulson
had come into a tidy inheritance and a business that never
ran short of customers for long. So had that father before
him and the sire's sire, for that matter. Goulson's Funeral
Parlor was one of the oldest established enterprises in the
county, and Harry Goulson took pride in his heritage.
Why should he dishonor the family name and risk his
professional standing by finagling a bribe he didn't need?

Was he having a love affair with Persephone Mink? Not
a chance, Shandy thought. He wouldn't dare, being
married to an accomplished, professional snoop like
Arabella. Besides, Persephone Mink was a virtuous woman. Shandy had it on Mrs. Betsy Lomax's personal authority that not another housewife in the village could shine a
copper saucepan like Sephy Mink. So dedicated a pan
polisher would hardly find time for clandestine amours.

What would Goulson want another woman for, anyway?
Arabella was a good-looker, a lively talker without being
tiresome, a snappy dresser without being flashy, a compe-
tent housekeeper, and a capable assistant. When it came to
putting the finishing touches on a loved one, Goulson
relied absolutely on Arabella's taste and artistry. Could he
throw such a talent to the winds?

Mrs. Goulson had presented her spouse with only one
child. That wasn't due to lack of connubial devotion,
though, but to female troubles vaguely alluded to by Mrs.

Lomax. Besides, the boy was as fine a lad as one would meet in a month of Sundays, zealous to follow in his forefathers' footsteps, and going steady with Lizanne Porble, of whom even the most doting parent would be hard put to disapprove. Goulson had always appeared satisfied with his lot in life. As far as Shandy could see, he damned well ought to be.

If Harry Goulson hadn't lied for love or money, might he not still have done so out of kindness? Looking around this discouraged little place, thinking of the three old people, Sephy's parents and Purvis's aunt, who'd needed a roof over their heads and probably hadn't the price of a bag of shingle nails to keep it on with, Shandy could understand why Persephone might be drawn into a scheme to extract money from the college, especially if there was any shred of evidence that the Trevelyan Bugginses might have something like a legitimate claim.

Sephy wouldn't be doing it for herself, Goulson would realize that. Purvis Mink made a decent week's pay. Their children had been eligible to attend the college tuition-free. Two of the daughters had studied with Mrs. Mouzouka, opened a coffee shop near the soap works in Lumpkinton, and done just fine. They'd started another in Hoddersville and sold both for a good price when their husbands got transferred. Mrs. Lomax had told Professor Shandy all about the Mink girls one day when he'd stayed home to grade papers on the mistaken assumption that he'd be able to work there in peace and quiet.

So the Minks ought to be sitting pretty, but maybe for some reason they weren't. Shandy wouldn't know, but Goulson would. Between Arabella's work for the *Fane and Pennon* and Harry's membership in all the local clubs and lodges, the Goulsons didn't miss much. Even now, with her parents beyond any earthly need, Persephone might feel too deeply committed to draw back from whatever scheme was afoot, and Goulson might understand why.

But this was no time to stand around speculating. Miss Minerva Mink, for it must be she, was peeking out at them through the mended lace curtain on the front door. How the blue blazes was he going to work around to asking her whether she thought Mrs. and Mrs. Buggins could have been murdered?

Chapter 5

S handy cleared his throat and raised his hat. "Miss Mink?"

The woman standing in the doorway answered him by a weary nod. Everything about her seemed tired. No wonder, Shandy thought, considering the kind of morning she'd had thus far. He had a hunch, though, that Miss Mink always looked tired.

She was wearing a longish dress of some limp gray material with a gray worsted cardigan over it. The dress wasn't exactly shabby and certainly not unclean, but it drooped from her lean frame as if it had known from the start there was no earthly use of its ever pretending to be stylish.

Everything about Miss Mink drooped, for that matter: her shoulders, her spine, the end of her thin nose, the wrinkles hacked into her grayish face by a mouth that must have developed a permanent downturn about three-score years ago. Her stockings were gray, and bagged. Her black shoes were what everybody's grandmother used to wear when Shandy was a boy: laced-up oxfords with Cuban heels. Most women wouldn't call them Cuban anymore, Shandy supposed, but he'd bet Miss Mink still did. He essayed another courtesy.

"I expect you know Chief Ottermole, and this is Cronkite Swope of the *Weekly Fane and Pennon*. We dropped by to, er, pay our respects."

"You can pay your respects at Goulson's Funeral Parlor

tomorrow from two to four and seven to nine," she told him in a voice as gray as her stockings. "No member of the family is present to receive visitors."

Miss Mink started to close the door. Shandy took hold of the knob from the outside. "Actually, what we came for is—"

"I know what you came for." Her tone didn't change. "You came to talk Persephone out of the lawsuit. You ought to be ashamed of yourself, Frederick Ottermole, abetting this minion of the vested interests against the workers of the earth."

"Huh? Who? Him?" Miss Mink's reprimand had clearly shaken the police chief. Shandy wondered if she'd been Ottermole's fourth-grade teacher. "Are you whatever she said, Professor?"

"I said he's a grinder of the faces of the poor," Miss Mink amplified, still without any enthusiasm.

"No, you didn't." Ottermole had got his nerve back. "You said something about a minion in a vest. An' you said Purve an' Sephy was workers of the earth, which they ain't. Purve's a security guard, an' Sephy hates to garden 'cause she's scared to death of bees."

"I was speaking figuratively," Miss Mink droned, but Fred Ottermole wasn't having any figures.

"Whereas," he brought out the word with visible pride, "what the professor does mostly is raise turnips when he's not being what you might call my unofficial deputy. Seeing as how I got hardly no regular force except Budge Dorkin, I have to make do with what I can get, which I wouldn't if people would get out an' vote me enough money to run my station with. How long since you been to town meeting, Miss Mink?"

She gave him a look. Her eyes were a pale, watery blue, Shandy noticed, like the unidentified corpse's.

"Now, don't you start in on me, Frederick. You know perfectly well I couldn't just waltz out of here as the whim seized me and leave Mr. and Mrs. Buggins to fend for themselves. I had to do my duty in the sphere of life to which I was called, didn't I? And what's to become of me now?" she finished bleakly.

"Well, heck, Purve an' Sephy—"

"Already have Purvis's mother living with them—and will have until the end of her days, if I know Rosalinda Mink."

"So what? They got two spare bedrooms now the kids are all gone."

"I find it impossible to visualize any house large enough to hold both myself and Rosalinda. And to think I might have been living in my own snug home all this time, if only I hadn't been stupid enough to let good nature prevail over common sense."

For the first time, Miss Mink's voice quivered with bona fide emotion. "How sadly do I rue the day I let my handsome cousin Algernon talk me into signing over my share of the old home so Aunt Amelia could, as he put it, live out her years in peace knowing she'd always have a roof over her head. Next thing I knew, Algernon had gambled away the property, Aunt Amelia was over the hill to the poorhouse, and I was out in the cold."

The down-drooping lips tightened into a thin gray line. "If Persephone Mink fails to profit from my disastrous example, she's a bigger fool than I take her for. And so I told her. Demand your rights, Sephy, I said. You never know. Purvis appears healthy enough, but they're always the first to go. He'll drop down dead in his tracks one day, I said, and then where will you be? Sephy didn't like that much, I have to tell you, but I reminded her she'd like it a good deal less trotting into the county welfare office and admitting she's a pauper."

"But she wouldn't be," Shandy protested. "All college personnel get free life insurance, and Mrs. Mink would be able to collect her husband's pension as long as she lived."

Minerva Mink sniffed. "The widow's mite."

"Then again, they mightn't. Hi, Min."

The interruption came from a flaming hulk of a woman with red-orange hair, red-purple cheeks, and scarlet lips painted on sideways in the manner of the late Pablo Picasso. She came wallowing around from behind the house in a pair of floppy rubber boots that had been splashed with red paint, perhaps in an effort to achieve the *tout ensemble*. Above them, she wore what Shandy assumed was a red dress, though he supposed it might be a red petticoat or simply an outsize red shirt. Whatever it was dragged in exuberant dips and swoops from under a dirty windbreaker she was clutching around her with her fists balled on the inside and the sleeves flapping empty, further distorting an already uncouth figure.

"Didn't know you was expectin' company, Min," she rasped around a cigarette that was stuck in the corner of her incarnadined mouth. "I just run over to see was there anything I could do."

Miss Mink jumped as though she'd been poked with a hat pin, stared at the apparition as if she couldn't imagine what it might be, then recovered her composure. She even managed a grim apology for a smile.

"You came to snoop, and what you can do for me is take yourself right back to where you came from. When I want any help from the likes of you, I'll ask for it, thank you very much."

"Huh. Try to be neighborly, an' where does it get you?" The neighbor glanced around from under her unkempt vermilion tresses, saw no welcome in the men's faces, and left.

Cronkite Swope, who'd been having some trouble with his nose, put away his tissues and essayed a change of subject. "What's this about a lawsuit, Miss Mink?"

"That is a family concern and none of yours, young man."

"Oh, come on, Miss Mink. You wouldn't hold out on a poor newspaperman with a living to earn?"

Cronkite Swope was withal an attractive young sprout, as half the winsome young ladies of Balaclava County would have been only too pleased to certify. Swope was perhaps wondering whether, where Cousin Algernon had once pulled a successful wheedle, he himself might yet succeed.

He might have, too, if he hadn't been interrupted by a car's driving into the yard just as he'd got his engaging grin up to full candlepower. The car was a newish American one in a discreet brown color, and Shandy wasn't surprised to see Persephone Mink driving. What did surprise him was that Grace Porble was with her.

Then Shandy remembered that Grace was not just the college librarian's wife but a Buggins in her own right. It was she who came first up the stairs.

"How are you, Miss Mink? What a dreadful thing to happen, both Uncle Trev and Auntie Bea in the same night. I suppose it's better this way, but it's still a shock. Why, Peter Shandy! Whatever are you doing here?"

"Exerting undue influence is the word, I believe," Miss Mink answered before Shandy could get a word in edgewise. "Or trying to. He came about the lawsuit."

"Aunt Minerva," cried Persephone, "you haven't been talking about that in front of a reporter?"

Both Grace and Persephone shied away from Cronkite Swope as if he were a bad case of the flu. Miss Mink shook her tidy gray head.

"All I said was it's nobody's business but the family's."

Grace Porble sighed. "I wish you hadn't said anything at all. Phil's upset enough already."

"I don't see what call he has to fret himself," Miss Mink snapped back. "He doesn't stand to make anything out of it."

"Well, Purve's none too happy, either," said Persephone.

"I don't know what we're standing out here on the doorstep for. Come inside, Aunt Minerva. You'd better sit down before you fall down."

She put her arm around the gray worsted cardigan and led her husband's aunt into the house. Grace Porble lingered beside Peter Shandy.

"Peter," she murmured, glancing over to make sure Cronkite Swope wasn't trying to eavesdrop, which he wasn't, being a well-brought-up young man. Fred Ottermole was, but Grace gave him a look, and he backed off. "Peter, what are you really doing here?"

"I'm on an errand for the president, if you want to know. Didn't your cousin tell you about the man who wasn't her brother?"

"The one you and Fred Ottermole fished out of Oozak's Pond? Surely you don't think that has anything to do with this? Peter Shandy, if you start trying to make a scandal out of the way Sephy's parents died, I'll strangle you with my bare hands."

"Drat it, Grace, I'm not trying to make anything out of anything. Look, we'd better talk later on, when you're free. I hadn't realized you were such pals with Mrs. Mink."

"Sephy and I are some kind of cousins. Helen could tell you in what degree, I expect. I can't. Anyway, we've always been fond of each other. We even lived together before we got married, in that little house where those two associate professors, Pam Waggoner and Shirley Wrenne, live now. Spinsters' Haven, they used to call it, but don't tell Shirley that. Peter, I've got to go in. Get that Swope boy out of here before he prints something about the family."

"Grace, you know he's going to do that, anyway. Why don't you spike his guns by giving him a few decorous facts for the obituary?"

"Oh, all right. I suppose I'd better."

None too happily, the librarian's wife went over to the reporter and began outlining the meager highlights of her deceased relatives' undistinguished lives. Shandy took advantage of her preoccupation to slip inside the house.

The old Buggins place looked about the way he'd expected it to, clean and dejected, like Miss Mink's gray dress. The rooms were tiny, the floors sagged. The furniture hadn't been much good to start with and hadn't been improved by the passage of time. There were too many crocheted doilies, too many knickknacks and doo-dads, too much varnished woodwork and faded wallpaper, too many yellowed photographs, not enough light and air, and definitely no sign of welcome on the faces turned toward him as he entered the parlor where Mrs. and Miss Mink were standing.

"Er, sorry to trouble you, ladies. Grace is talking to Swope about the obituary. She sent me to get a photograph of Mr. and Mrs. Buggins for the paper. She said you'd know which one."

To Shandy's relief, both women accepted his barefaced lie. "I suppose Grace means the one Arabella Goulson took at their fiftieth wedding anniversary," said Persephone. "Do you know where it is, Aunt Minerva?"

"I expect your mother kept it upstairs in her top dresser drawer, but I'm not going up there to get it. Mrs. Buggins was always touchy about the hired help prying into her personal affairs."

"Aunt Minerva, you were never hired help."

"Then would you kindly and gently tell me what I was?"

Persephone sighed and went to fetch the photograph. Arabella Goulson had made an attractive presentation of it in a deckle-edged cardboard folder, but she hadn't been able to do much with her subjects. The cake they were cutting was impressively decorated, the outfits they wore must have been bought new for the occasion, but the couple inside the clothes were such pallid wisps that they seemed hardly more than a vague excuse for the fancy confectionery, the corsage, and the boutonnière. Shandy

wondered how this puny pair had ever managed to produce a daughter like Persephone, let alone twin sons.

Among the clutter on the mantelpiece, he spied a picture of the boys, perhaps taken for the high school graduation Bainbridge hadn't waited to attend. They did look
alike but, as Harry Goulson had said, not so alike that you
couldn't tell them apart when you got them together. Both
had the Buggins nose and chin. If they'd grown beards as
they got older, either one of them might have resembled
Balaclava Buggins as much as the man in the pond had.

Too bad it was a black-and-white photo, hence there was
no telling what the eye color might have been. The eyes
didn't look dark enough to have been brown, but the
photograph had no doubt faded considerably after all
these years. And Goulson had described the eyes as hazel,
which might have meant almost anything.

Miss Mink cleared her throat, reminding Shandy of
what he was allegedly there for. "Is that the picture you
wanted?"

"Oh, yes," he stuttered. "This will, er, do just, er, fine.
Devoted couple, weren't they? It must have been a
dreadful shock to you, Miss Mink, finding them both, er,
together. Though, since Mrs. Buggins had been ill with
pneumonia—"

"Mother didn't have pneumonia," Persephone interrupted sharply. "If she had, we'd have taken her to the
hospital."

"But I understand Dr. Fotheringay gave the cause of, er,
passing as respiratory failure. That means pneumonia,
doesn't it?"

"It means she stopped breathing when she died. People
generally do."

"I see. And your father's was heart failure."

"Just so."

"Which is to say also that people's hearts generally stop
beating once they quit breathing. How right you are, Mrs.

Mink. Did Mr. Buggins have a history of coronary weakness?"

"No, as a matter of fact, the last time Papa had a checkup, Dr. Fotheringay said—" Persephone stopped short and tightened her mouth. "Thank you for stopping by, Professor Shandy. The funeral's half past eight Wednesday morning at the First Church, if you'd care to come."

Chapter 6

Helen Shandy laid down the sandwich she'd been eating and glared at her husband across the kitchen table. "Peter, I cannot possibly go pumping Grace Porble when she's in the midst of a family funeral. Anyway, I wouldn't be able to get hold of her. She's all tied up with poor Sephy."

"What do you mean, poor Sephy? I didn't know you were on Sephying terms with Purvis Mink's wife."

"Of course I am. Sephy's in the garden club, isn't she?"

"If you say so," Shandy replied, sneaking Jane Austen a sliver of chicken from his own sandwich.

"I saw that, Peter Shandy. You know perfectly well Jane isn't supposed to be fed at the table."

The small tiger cat jumped up into Helen's lap and began washing her white whiskers with a white-mittened paw. Helen rubbed one finger along Jane's delicate jaw.

"And so do you, you little scrounger. Grace is terribly upset over Sephy's parents, Peter. She's canceled the Bonsai Workshop out of respect."

"Good gad, I hadn't realized the far-reaching ramifications of this unfortunate occurrence."

Helen got up, ostensibly to refill the teapot, actually to come around the table and lay a wifely hand on Shandy's shoulder. "Darling, you're not going to make trouble for Grace and Sephy, are you?"

Disregarding Jane's designs on his sandwich, Shandy stood up and put his arms around Helen. "I don't know

52

yet if there's any trouble to be made. The medical examiner's due at Goulson's sometime soon. I hope he'll find both parents' deaths were due to natural causes."

"Why shouldn't he?" said Helen. "Couldn't Mr. Buggins have waked up in the night, found his wife dead in bed beside him, and had a heart attack from the shock?"

"Certainly he could. It's also possible that stiff we fished out of the pond this morning dressed up as Augustus Buggins, filled his pockets with rocks, and jumped into Oozak's Pond just for the hell of it. What sticks in my craw is that all three bodies have turned up at the same time as Ichabod Buggins's descendants are threatening the college with a lawsuit over the water rights from the pond."

"Whatever are you talking about?"

Shandy explained, in words that ranged from the mildly profane to the downright scatological. Helen listened, first aghast, then bitter.

"So our precious president's dumped the mess into your lap, as usual. I wish Thorkjeld Svenson would go fly a kite."

"No doubt he would, if you asked him nicely."

"You needn't try to be funny."

Helen disentangled herself from his embrace and picked up the cat. "Come to Mummy, Jane. We women have to stick together at a time like this. I'm warning you, Peter, if it turns out Sephy Mink is entitled to a legitimate share in Oozak's Pond—"

"Then you'd better learn how to dip tallow candles, because that's what you'll be doing the Buggins family history by the light of," Shandy finished for her. "In point of fact, the president has not dumped this mess exclusively into my lap. A goodly chunk of it's in yours. Svenson expects us to work as a team. Any information that could bail the college out of a lawsuit ought to be in the archives, and you're the only one with the expertise to dig it out.

You'll probably find an official ukase on your desk when you get back to the library."

"Dr. Porble's going to be in an awful swivet."

"He's in one already," Shandy assured his wife. "Grace was telling Miss Mink this morning how burned up Phil is over the lawsuit. She sounded pretty bedraggled herself."

"Poor Grace, why wouldn't she be? Dr. Porble's all for the college, no doubt, as you yourself would be, and she's on Sephy's side. So am I, but not very far on. After all, Sephy wasn't my bridesmaid."

It had been Sieglinde Svenson herself who'd taken on that function and served a nice smorgasbord with seven kinds of herring afterward, to make sure the erstwhile maverick Peter Shandy was well and duly corralled. Sieglinde must be on one side or the other, too, but she'd be far too suave a diplomat to let anybody know which. Still, it was clear there'd be a good many divided loyalties and perhaps a full-scale civil war before the ownership of Oozak's Pond got straightened out, assuming it ever did.

"Drat," Shandy exploded. "I wish that corpse had turned out to be Bracebridge Buggins. You don't suppose Persephone Mink could have been wrong about the identification?"

"Sephy's never wrong about anything," said Helen. "Ask anybody. Peter, dear, have you stopped to consider that since Dr. Porble had been chewing Grace's ear about the lawsuit when you saw her this morning and that since Thorkjeld didn't throw his fit until after he'd been to his office and read his mail, then the Porbles must have known some time before he did?"

"I have stopped to consider, yes. Obviously, Persephone Mink had to be aware of what was up some time ago. Lawyers' letters don't get written overnight. There must have been considerable discussion among the family before they took any action, and it's hard to believe she wasn't involved in that. Being so close to Grace, who's also a relative, Persephone would naturally have let her know about the lawsuit."

"And Grace would have told Dr. Porble, and Sephy must surely have told Purvis. They're a very devoted couple, I believe."

Like Trevelyan and Beatrice. "I wonder how devoted Purvis Mink would be to the prospect of risking a good, steady job with assured benefits and a generous pension by participating in a wildcat scheme to gouge money out of the institution that provides the job, the benefits, and the pension," said Shandy.

"Not terribly keen, I suppose," Helen admitted. "Purvis loves his job, Sephy says, particularly when he works the night shift. He gets a kick out of watching the owls."

"*Chacun à son goût*," said Shandy, who was a hawk man himself. "I suppose Persephone was beguiled into this harebrained lawsuit by the lure of easy money, but I can't understand why Purvis didn't try to head her off."

"Sephy wouldn't be lured by easy money."

"Well, drat it, she must have been lured by something."

"Family pride, I suppose. Darling, can't you imagine what it must have been like for a girl who was supposed to be connected with the local aristocracy, growing up in that ratty old house without two nickels to rub together and having to wear Grace's hand-me-downs? Grace used to pretend they swapped clothes back and forth because they were cousins, but everybody knew Sephy wouldn't have had a rag to her name if it hadn't been for Grace."

"Who told you that?"

"I have my sources."

"Mrs. Lomax, I suppose. So now Sephy's out for revenge?

"I expect she'd call it getting a little of her own back. Put yourself in Sephy's place, Peter. If your people had been the underdogs generation after generation and your parents were old and discouraged, and suddenly they thought they'd found a way to get up on top at last, wouldn't you have a hard time refusing to back them up?"

"And Grace is willing to stand behind her, even though the parents are dead?"

"How do I know where Grace is standing? Right now I daresay she's trying to stay neutral about the lawsuit and help Sephy cope with the funeral. It's an awful spot for her to be in."

Unless Sephy decided to drop the lawsuit, Shandy thought. If not, the situation could only get worse. Phil Porble must be doing some heavy thinking about now. If he found after due deliberation that justice lay on Persephone's side, he'd support her regardless of the consequences to himself, Grace, or the college. If he decided the Ichabod Buggins claim was a bundle of horsefeathers, he wouldn't hesitate to start a family feud by saying so. If he'd already determined that some action on his own part was required to solve the dilemma, Phil would act. Whether his dispassionate logic would lead him to drown the man who thought up the lawsuit, Shandy honestly didn't know.

"Peter, I know what you're thinking, and he wouldn't," said Helen. "He wouldn't have to. If he wanted to get rid of somebody, he'd just give them one of his looks and they'd wither away."

"M'well, you know Porble better than I do, I suppose, notwithstanding the fact that he and I had been colleagues for approximately eighteen years before you ever got here."

"Bah, humbug. You may have strolled into the library to look up petunia statistics occasionally or to give him a hard time about opening up the Buggins Room on the off chance there'd be a copy of the collected poems of John G. Saxe you could get your lustful hands on. That's not knowing."

"Not knowing in the sense that I couldn't tell you what

color pajamas he wears, perhaps. That seems to be the sort of thing women always seem to think matters."

"I haven't the remotest idea what color pajamas Dr. Porble wears, nor have I troubled to inquire," Helen retorted icily. "Probably cream-colored silk with a tasteful maroon piping and his initials embroidered on the pocket. Darn you, Peter, why did you have to mention pajamas? Now I'll wonder about them next time I see him. And get an unseemly fit of the giggles, like as not."

"You might more profitably expend your wonderment on why two more or less identical corpses turned up in Oozak's Pond eighty years apart," Shandy suggested. "Who besides yourself and Phil Porble has access to the Buggins Archive? You don't let visitors wander at will through the Buggins Room, do you?"

"You know perfectly well we don't."

For half a century or more, the Buggins Room had been a dusty, cobwebbed dump for splintered crates nobody wanted to look through. Now all books were shelved according to the Dewey decimal system, all papers dealt with according to the Helen Marsh Shandy system.

Helen had gone ferreting in the library basement and found a long oak table, which she'd caused to be lugged upstairs by a squad of burly sophomores for the better sorting and collating of the Buggins Archive. By now, the table was covered with racks and baskets full of carefully annotated folders that scholars from other areas were itching to get a look at. Dr. Porble himself, having for decades despised and ignored the Buggins Collection as an incubus that took up space better devoted to hog statistics, was virtually being forced to take an interest.

He could easily have taken advantage of his position as library director and keeper of the extra key to wander in and poke around. He could have come upon Corydon's memorial ode to Augustus, read it, and returned it to its designated spot without Helen's ever knowing, now that she was doing much of her work at home. Later, faced with the problem of dispatching a pestiferous Buggins and remembering what Henry Doe had got away with, his sardonic sense of humor might conceivably have prompted him to try Doe's method again.

Helen wasn't ready to ascribe such perfidy to her boss. "Dr. Porble wouldn't do a thing like that," she insisted. "Anyway, lots of people might have heard the story. It's the sort of yarn grandparents like to scare their grandchildren with."

"True enough," he replied. "Can't you see little Gracie Buggins listening wide-eyed to Uncle Trevelyan spinning the tale, with her pigtails standing right up straight and her kitty cat purring by her side? And passing it on to Phil during their courting days while they strolled hand in hand around picturesque old Oozak's Pond watching the bullfrogs seduce the cowfrogs."

"Grace and Phil would have been doing no such thing. They'd be over at the library, necking in the stacks. Grace told me so. She said she and Phil were always catching students at it, and they thought they might as well try it themselves in the spirit of scholarly research. Phil was rooming with some old battle-ax down on Grove Street at the time. His landlady used to wait up for him, to make sure he hadn't taken to drink or moral turpitude. He'd stroll in about half past eleven with lipstick all over his shirtfront and try to make her believe he'd been sorting Library of Congress catalog cards."

"Good gad, a master of deceitful dalliance and carnal cunning! Why couldn't they go and canoodle in the cottage? Weren't Grace and Persephone living there then?"

"Yes, but Sephy was already going steady with Purvis Mink. Purvis had ten or eleven brothers and sisters at home, so they could hardly go to his house. And naturally Sephy wouldn't invite him out to her folks' because it was so awfully depressing and her father would insist on telling them all the corny old stories she'd heard a million times already."

"The one about the corpse in Oozak's Pond, for instance."

"All right, Peter, you've made your point."

Persephone Buggins would surely have heard about Augustus's watery doom and passed it on to Grace if nobody else did. Being a collateral connection of Corydon's, Trevelyan would no doubt have held on to a copy of his poems. Scions of old families who've hit the skids do like to flaunt their illustrious ancestors, and Corydon Buggins had evidently cut as grand a figure on the Balaclava County literary scene as Charles Follen Adams or even Lydia Sigourney had done in wider circles.

Shandy snorted at such once-famous names. "In my opinion, Belial Buggins could rhyme the pants off the lot of them."

"I'm not saying he couldn't," Helen had to agree, "but you must admit, Belial's verses weren't the sort young ladies could copy into their albums."

"Belial was a man ahead of his time."

"He was usually about three jumps ahead of some irate husband carrying a shotgun, too."

"So he was. Damn, I wish old Hilda Horsefall hadn't moved to Sweden. She'd know how many of Belial's bastard begets passed on the family genes and which of their children favor the Bugginses as much as that bearded enigma on Goulson's mortuary slab does. Maybe Mrs. Lomax can tell."

"She might tell me, but she'd never tell you," said Helen. "She's much too delicate in the sensibilities to discuss such things with a man she isn't married to. The problem is, she'll know why I'm asking, and she'll tie it straight up with the Minks. Mrs. Lomax wouldn't breathe a word that might hurt Purvis and Sephy."

"Gad! The schism is widening faster than you can shake a stick at it," Shandy groaned.

"You can't shake a stick at a schism, dear. At least I suppose you could, but I can't see what you'd accomplish if you did. Were you planning to walk me back up to the library, or shall I try to make it on my own?"

"Why? Do you feel a swoon coming on?"

"I suppose that means you'd rather get back to Goulson's and hang out with the medical examiner."

"Wouldn't you rather I hung out with him than hung from Svenson's paws as a bleeding pulp?"

"Oh, all right, if you're squeamish about getting mangled. I'll see if I can find anything about Oozak's Pond among Balaclava's personal records, but there's an awful lot to get through. I must say this lawsuit sounds totally spurious to me, Peter. Ichabod was Balaclava's nephew, you know."

"You said Dalbert was Balaclava's nephew."

"There were four nephews. Dalbert was the only son of Balaclava's sister, Druella, who married Fortitude Lumpkin and founded Lumpkin Corners. Ichabod, Corydon, and Belial were sons of Balaclava's brother, Abelard, the horse trader. Abelard built that house where Trevelyan and Beatrice lived as a wedding present for Ichabod when he married Prudence Plover in 1831. Prudence was said to be a little weak in the head, though that may have been only because she had no more sense than to marry Ichabod."

"Who never amounted to much."

"Right. Corydon, on the other hand, took over his father's horse-trading business and did very well at it, when he wasn't being visited by an attack of the muse. Belial got disinherited for reasons too numerous to mention but didn't care because he had his own sources of income."

"And could always find a bed for the night."

"Don't digress. I don't know how we got started on nephews. What I meant to say was that Balaclava Buggins was a sensible, dedicated man. He taught school before he was sixteen, he farmed, he lived what he preached. He truly believed in earning his bread by the sweat of his brow and training young people to be good farmers and good citizens. He knew perfectly well the only way he could reach them was by setting an example worth following. Does that sound like the kind of man who'd go around making reckless bets?"

"Not to me, but I doubt if you're going to sell an unsupported argument to the Bugginses' lawyers. Or to Miss Minerva Mink."

"Miss Mink? What does she have to do with the lawsuit?"

"Good question. She claims to have been bilked of her patrimony and maybe also of her matrimony by her handsome cousin Algernon and is determined not to let Persephone make a similar mistake. Miss Mink doesn't talk as if she carried much clout among the Bugginses, but one never knows. Come on, I'll walk you back to the library before I go to Goulson's."

Chapter 7

"**S**o what's the verdict?" Shandy asked.

"Interesting," said the medical examiner. "With all respect to the doctor who made out the death certificate, the old man's heart must have been remarkably sound, considering his age, and the old lady's lungs as clear as a bell. And vice versa, I may add. If Chief Ottermole doesn't mind, I'd like to take some bits and pieces back for analysis."

"Take all you want," said the chief. "They won't be needing them anymore. How about the guy we fished out of the pond?"

"A straightforward case of murder."

"Huh? How come not suicide? Couldn't he simply have filled his pockets with rocks to weigh him down an' jumped in?"

"Not after somebody ran an ice pick into the base of his skull, he couldn't. In fact, I'm wondering if he may have been left lying around somewhere for a day or two before he was put into the pond. There are certain signs not altogether consistent with immediate immersion in icy water and none whatever of drowning."

"Then one person acting alone may have killed him and had to wait some time for help in dumping the body, do you think?" said Shandy.

"It's a possibility. He may have been driven across country in a car with a heater running, for all I know, though I can't imagine why. I'm not saying the weapon was in fact an ice pick, but an ice pick would have made exactly the kind of wound he received. Driving it into his neck wouldn't have taken any great amount of strength if it was sharp enough, which it obviously was. Getting a tall, well-nourished corpse into the pond would have taken more than average strength and was most likely done by more than one person. Unless he was considerate enough to be lying facedown on a toboggan when he was stabbed."

"With his pockets full of rocks."

"You do slay with panache over here, I must say. Could you lend me a couple of buckets for the stomachs, Goulson?"

"Better bring a spare," mumbled Fred Ottermole. They weren't actually in the room where the autopsy had been taking place, but they were closer to it than he wished he were. Ottermole was still suffering from the morning's injudicious combination of corpse and crullers.

Seeing a relapse on the way, Shandy hastened to change the subject. "What can you tell us about the murdered man, Doctor? We still don't have an identification, as Goulson must have told you, and we'd welcome any ideas you may have. Did you get any, er, Holmesian hints from his hands, for instance?"

"Well, he wasn't a surgeon or a golfer." The coroner displayed his own calluses as evidence. "He may have done a fair amount of physical labor when he was younger, but not all that much in recent years. He was in excellent physical condition for a man his age, which would be between sixty and sixty-five, I'd say; well nourished but not fat, didn't smoke or drink to excess, and spent a lot of time outdoors. He might possibly have been a construction foreman who'd worked his way up from the pick-and-shovel brigade or something on that general line, but that's only a guess."

"What about his teeth?"

"They'd been freshly pulled. By an amateur using a hammer and chisel, from the looks of the gums."

"My God! To hamper identification, I suppose."

"Oh, yes. The fingertips have been sandpapered, too. Quite a home handyman's job all around. I haven't had time to prowl through that beard, but I'd suggest you have Goulson get rid of it. There may be a scar or birthmark underneath that would give you a clue. We took some pictures of him all nicely dried and combed out before I began my examination, by the way."

"We got some, too," Fred Ottermole bragged. "We had a photographer on the scene when we hauled him out of the pond."

"By George, Chief Ottermole, you're an organizer. I don't see how you run such a tight department with such a tiny staff, the lowest budget in the county, and the highest percentage of murders."

"We got no more murders than any place else," Ottermole protested. "It's just that we don't pussyfoot around calling 'em what they ain't. Chief Olson over at Lumpkinton, he finds a body with six bullets in it, tied up with clothesline, an' stuffed into an old icebox. There's six fresh holes shot through the icebox door, an' he tries to pass it off as suicide while of unsound mind because the stiff's his wife's cousin's brother-in-law."

"That was carrying family loyalty to the ultimate limit," the medical examiner agreed. "Speaking of families and identifications, Professor Shandy, have you noticed how strongly the man we've been talking about resembles the late Mr. Buggins? Perhaps it's not obvious at first glance because of the difference in age and size and all that facial hair, but the bone structure, the shape of the ears, and, of course, the eye color are remarkably similar."

"The eye color?" said Shandy. "You mean that washed-out blue? I never knew the Bugginses. What color were the wife's eyes?"

"Why, I can't say I noticed particularly. Harry, can you enlighten us?"

The undertaker hesitated. "Sort of hazely, aren't they?"

"Let's go take a look," said Shandy.

Fred Ottermole gulped. "I got to call the station."

"Why don't you go out in the side hall and use the phone down near the rest rooms?" Harry Goulson suggested kindly. "I'll just run ahead and get the loved ones ready for viewing, you not being much used to autopsies."

Peter Shandy was grateful that Goulson's preparation had included covering the three corpses with sheets, all but their faces. The eyes were open. He took a look at Beatrice Buggins's and shook his head. "Is that what you call hazel, Goulson?"

"If you want the honest truth, Professor, I always say hazel unless they're plain blue or brown. I'm not much on colors. Arabella picks out the clothes and does the makeup mostly. What would you call them?"

"I'd say darkish gray. Do you agree, Doctor?"

"Yes, I do. To me, hazel suggests a tinge of brown, and I don't see any of that here. Rather an unusual shade, isn't it? She must have been pretty when she was young. Well, if we're through here, I'll get back to the lab and see what else I can find out for you. I may have some information on the stomach contents by the end of the afternoon. You can handle things here, can't you, Harry?"

"Sure thing, Doctor. Let me give you a hand with those buckets."

Chief Ottermole came out of the men's room and said he had urgent business over at the station, which nobody doubted for a moment. Shandy was reminded that he had to get to the bank before it closed or there'd be no money in the house to buy Jane Austen her supper. He left, too, deep in thought.

So Goulson's corroboration of Sephy Mink's statement about her brothers' brown eyes didn't amount to a hill of beans. The twins' eyes could have been dark gray like their mother's easily enough, but there was only one way they could have been brown, even a hazel brown.

Shandy was of course familiar with Mendel's experiments in color dominance among plants and with the vast body of work that has since been done. He was a trifle hazy about eye color in humans, but he was pretty damned certain a blue-eyed man and a gray-eyed woman could never have produced brown-eyed twins without a little help from a brown-eyed friend.

The Bugginses were alleged to have been a devoted couple, but people always said that about any pair who'd managed to stick it out together for over fifty years. In defense of Beatrice Buggins's fidelity, however, there was that strong family resemblance between the two male corpses. Drat! Persephone must either have forgotten what color her brothers' eyes were or else had not forgotten and was trying to cover up a suspicious death, like Chief Olson with the in-law in the icebox.

On the other hand, suppose Persephone had forgotten and was not lying. Did that mean the college was stuck with an authentic reincarnation of Augustus Caesar Buggins? How the flaming perdition was Peter Shandy going to explain a mudered supernatural phenomenon to Thorkjeld Svenson? Maybe he'd better go home, get Helen to pack her bags and Jane her catnip mouse, and flee with them to some relatively safe, peaceful spot, like the upper slopes of Mount St. Helen's.

After thinking the matter over, Shandy did go home, first pausing at the bank to restock his wallet; dispensing some of his cash at the grocery store on replenishments for the larder in case they decided to stay and ride out the storm, and having a few terse words with a student he happened to meet there on the subject of an overdue term paper. He found Helen in the kitchen making tapioca custard.

"It's soothing to the nerves," she explained. "Also to the eyeballs. Between that pale-brown ink and Balaclava's scratchy penmanship, I'm Bugginsed out. He must have beaten his nibs into plowshares."

"You haven't come across anything in the archives?"

"Not yet, but there's still a long way to go. Stir this for me, will you? Don't stop or it will curdle. I meant to bring up a jar of those cherry preserves we made last fall. Mary Enderble puts a layer in the bottom of the dish with a little rum and pours the hot tapioca over the cherries. It's lovely."

Shandy's culinary education had come a long way since the soup-heating days of his bachelorhood. However, Helen had never left him alone before with something that might take a pettish notion to curdle if you didn't treat it right. He was pushing the spoon in a careful rhythm, watching with incipient panic for any sign of a lump, when the telephone rang.

Luckily, the kitchen extension wasn't far from the stove. By holding the spoon by the tip and stretching as far as he could, Shandy was able to take down the receiver without having to pause. By the time Helen had got back upstairs with the cherries, though, the pudding had not only curdled but scorched, and Shandy hadn't even noticed.

"Oh, Peter!" That was as close to a rebuke as Helen got. "Peter, what's the matter?"

"Your friend Sephy's parents," he told her. "Ottermole just got the report. Somebody served them a nightcap. Moonshine and carbon tetrachloride."

Chapter 8

Helen stood staring at him with the cherries in her hand. "Carbon tetrachloride? Peter, that's cleaning fluid. Wouldn't the smell alone have put them off?"

"Maybe they couldn't smell it. Ottermole says Trevelyan Buggins kept up a family tradition by running his own still. He claims Buggins made the awfullest rotgut ever distilled in Balaclava County, and that's saying plenty. I reminded him carbon tet smells like chloroform, and he said old Trev's booze always smelled like chloroform. Besides, they'd had potatoes and onions fried in salt pork for supper. That must have stunk up the house pretty thoroughly and also made a cozy bed for the poison to work in. According to the medical examiner, fats in the digestive system would have speeded up the toxic effect. So would the alcohol. Whoever slipped them the slug must have known his chemistry."

"I'd say she must have planned the menu," said Helen.

"Ottermole jumped on that angle, too, but Mrs. Ottermole says the Bugginses always had potatoes and onions fried in salt pork on Thursday nights. It's an old Seven Forks tradition, God knows why. She claims those Thursday night suppers were what made Persephone leave home."

"Has Ottermole talked to Sephy?"

"Not yet. He was eating his own supper when the call came in. Naturally he told his wife about the report, and she happened to recall Persephone's joking about the

Thursday night fried pork at some women's shindig. Would it have been your garden club?"

"No, Edna Mae won't join till her boys get old enough to leave. It was more likely somebody's baby shower. Peter, this is horrible. You don't suppose the Bugginses were carrying out a suicide pact?"

"Just when they were about to restore the descendants of Ichabod Buggins to their place in the sun and wallow in unwonted wealth?"

"But what if they'd found out their claim was invalid and there wasn't gong to be any wealth?"

"They still wouldn't have been any worse off than they were before, would they?"

"I don't suppose so," Helen conceded. "They'd stick Sephy and Purvis for the lawyer's fee, no doubt. But it's so . . . so Ethan Frome-ish, those two old souls in that wretched house, toddling off to their long winter's nap with their tummies full of salt port and white lightning and never waking up. Though I suppose it would have been worse for them if they had."

"The medical examiner thinks they probably never did because they'd been given such a massive dose. If they did, they'd have had awful bellyaches, which they'd no doubt have put down to Miss Mink's cooking. Pretty soon they'd have felt drowsy again and passed out, and that would have been the end of them, unless they'd received immediate first aid."

"They wouldn't have called the doctor. They'd have taken paregoric or castor oil or something and just got sicker. Peter, that's diabolical."

"It's that, all right. Oddly enough, carbon tetrachloride can cause irregular heartbeat and respiratory failure. Even if he'd seen them alive, that doctor of theirs might still have diagnosed pneumonia and heart failure and had what seemed like good reasons for doing so. Maybe this is hardly the time to ask, but would you like a drink?"

"We'd better smell the cork first." Helen tried a shaky laugh, but it didn't come off. "Yes, I'll have one. Then what are you going to do?"

"Ottermole wants me to go out to First Fork with him right after supper, which I expect means roughly half an hour from now. He'll hate missing *Doctor Who,* but since he got that pat on the back from the medical examiner, he's all fired up about duty before pleasure."

"Provided you stand duty with him, I gather. There's no point in my setting the dining-room table, then. I'd meant to put on the dog a bit tonight so you wouldn't notice it's just warmed-over stew."

"All the better second time around," Shandy assured her. "And a damned sight better than potatoes fried in salt pork, though I've eaten enough of those in my time. Mother always kept salt pork in the icebox out at the farm. I remember watching my grandmother whacking off a piece to put in the bean pot on Saturday morning. And when she made fish hash, she'd try out a few slices in the big frying pan till they were nice and crispy, then crumble them in with the potatoes and onions and salt cod."

"I remember salt codfish. It came packed in little wooden boxes. I always wanted them for my doll's clothes, but the fish smell would never come out."

"Those boxes were for the aristocracy. What we had was just a hunk of fish, dried hard as a board and salty as a cattle lick. Grandma had to soak it overnight, then parboil it awhile to get out enough salt to make the fish palatable and soften it enough to break into flakes. She'd throw in plenty of black pepper and a beaten egg, cover the skillet, and set it on the back of the stove till it got a good brown crust on the bottom. It wasn't bad eating, with some homemade catsup to jazz it up a little."

"My mother used to cream the cod and serve it over boiled potatoes with hard-boiled eggs cut up in the sauce,"

Helen recalled. "I have to admit, I'd try to switch the plates around so I'd get more egg than fish."

"That's why you never grew any hair on your chest. Here you are, my love. Good for what ails you."

Shandy handed his wife her drink, knowing full well what ailed them both and why they were making small talk about codfish. "Were you planning to take another whack at the archives this evening?"

"I'll get back to work as soon as we've finished eating," Helen promised. "You're really pinning your faith to them, aren't you?"

"Faith is all I have so far, my love. Was Balaclava any sort of bookkeeper?"

"Compulsive. If he spent a penny for a postage stamp, down it went in the ledger."

"He wasn't the type to deed over a whole acre of land without at least jotting down a memorandum?"

"Not unless somebody swiped his ink pot. Even if they had, I expect he'd have brewed some more out of oak galls and iron filings or something. Balaclava was a great one for making the best use of everything, including people. It irked him terribly to see the brightest boys going off to be ministers or lawyers instead of sticking to the land and making it pay. He was absolutely wedded to the idea of an agricultural college, you know, even when he was still a teenager teaching a one-room school."

"Is all that in the archives?"

"It certainly is. Balaclava used to go on and on about his plan in his journals. He kept a diary right from the time he scraped together enough cash to buy his first quire of paper. His mother stitched the sheets together with needle and thread to make him a book. That's the most precious thing in the entire Buggins Collection, to my way of thinking. Balaclava never had literary aspirations, like his nephews Corydon and Belial, but he did have lots of ideas.

He liked to work things out on paper so he'd be all set to put them into practice when he got the chance."

"Then nothing but lack of money kept him from establishing the college long before 1850."

"That's right. His father could have helped but he wouldn't. Habakkuk Buggins wasn't one to pamper his sons with handouts during his lifetime. And when he died, he stuck to the old British custom of favoring the elder son. Abelard got the house and the best of the land, most of which his sons and grandson sold off or frittered away, as you know. All Balaclava got was this parcel out here in what was then considered the middle of nowhere. Habakkuk had picked it up for about two cents an acre, and most of his neighbors thought he'd got the short end of the deal. I'm sure you've heard all this before. More stew? Or some cherries without the tapioca?"

"Cherries, please. Go on about Balaclava."

"What I'm driving at is that his land was all Balaclava had. He couldn't bear to give up teaching, and he farmed on the side, as you know. That kept his family fed and clothed, but it didn't give him any working capital, so he made the land work for him. He sold off timber and fought for years to get the county road extended his way. Once he'd managed to push that through, he was able to attract a few tenant farmers, and the village began to evolve. This of course made his land more valuable, so he began selling off small parcels around the edges. By 1850, he was in a position to start building not only barns and dormitories but also houses he could rent or sell to his teachers. I don't have to tell you he wrote it right into the charter that the college was always to keep title to the land these houses stood on."

"By gad, yes. That's important, Helen. In lieu of anything specific about Oozak's Pond, a comprehensive statement of Balaclava's consistently farseeing policies with regard to his real estate might be enough to give the college the benefit of the doubt over this damned fool bet he's supposed to have lost. The hell of it is, there's always so much public sentiment in favor of the downtrodden private citizen up against the big, wicked institution."

"Those are generally your sentiments, too," Helen reminded him.

"Likewise yours, my love. But dag-nab it, in this case the college is the good guy. And I'm afraid it's up to you and me to establish that fact before any more Bugginses get done in and they hang the rap on Svenson. Here's wishing us luck. God knows we're going to need some."

He got into his old mackinaw, his storm boots, and his fleece-lined cap with the retractable earflaps. This wasn't what a person would call a good night, but it was not yet a noticeably bad one. With any luck, the snow flurries that had been piddling along since before daybreak would either give up and quit or else not develop into a full-scale storm until after he was back home and sound asleep.

He hoped the latter happy event would not be too long in occurring. This had been one of those days that set one to brooding on the futility of trying to measure off the hours with a clock. In theory, only twelve of them had elapsed since he'd stood up beside Oozak's Pond watching Beauregard ignore the multitude. Since then, the slothful groundhog had been back pounding his fuzzy ear in his presumably cozy den, while P. Shandy had been slogging knee-deep in slaughter. Shandy felt a savage impulse to go wake the little bastard up again.

Being a man of reason, however, he fought down the urge for vengeance and went to get his car. Now that he thought of it, why was he appointed chauffeur? Why wasn't Cronkite Swope slavering at their heels with the press car? Great balls of fire, was the intrepid newshound lying out in the dark somewhere with an ice pick through his neck?

Ottermole was able to reassure Shandy on that point,

though he first had to disentangle himself from his sons, who crowded the doorways yelling "Don't let the space monsters get you, Pop" before they rushed back to stimulate their budding intellects in front of the television set.

"Cronk's in bed sick" was his report. "He stopped off home to get a muffler 'cause he'd begun sneezing his head off from getting his feet wet up at the pond. His mother heard him an' wouldn't let him back out."

"I wonder if Charles Kuralt ever ran into a similar problem," Shandy mused as he turned up the old county road. "Am I correct in assuming we're headed toward First Fork?"

"Well, yeah. I figured we might as well go back an' arrest Miss Mink or somebody."

"Sounds like a great idea to me. Does Miss Mink drive a car?"

"Nope. I don't see where she ever had a chance to learn how. She never owned one herself, an' the Bugginses haven't had one since old Trev racked up his brand-new Edsel. He wanted to buy another, but Sephy an' Purve wouldn't sign the note for the loan. Trev never could remember which side of the road he was s'posed to drive on. Sephy or Purve always took him an' his wife anyplace they wanted to go. Miss Mink used to ride a bicycle, but she had to give it up on account of her sciatica."

"Too bad. By the way, what did Miss Mink do before she came to live with the Bugginses?"

"Took care of her own folks mostly. Then she stayed with the Sills for a while after Mrs. Sill got so she needed somebody in the house all the time, but I guess Miss Mink didn't get along too good with the congressman. They'd fight about politics. So she went on to the Bugginses', an' she's been there ever since."

"So, in fact, she's a, er, professional housekeeper-companion."

"I s'pose you could call her that."

Ottermole fell silent, perhaps worrying about what extraterrestrial peril might now be threatening Dr. Who, perhaps brooding over the ill-timed maternal solicitude that was keeping Cronkite Swope from taking pictures of him arresting Miss Mink or somebody.

Shandy let him brood. As for himself, he'd as soon see Miss Mink jugged as anybody, after the reception she'd given them this morning. She might be worth pinching, at that. She'd had every opportunity to kill the Bugginses. As for motive, mightn't a person get so fed up with a lifetime of making porridge for enfeebled oldsters that she'd do almost anything for a change?

Minerva Mink hadn't talked like an ignorant woman, but she'd made some fairly wild remarks. She could be a trifle touched, and she must at some time have had access to carbon tetrachloride.

It was only during the past few years that the dangerous chemical hadn't been sold openly as a cleaning agent. When she'd lived with the Sills, Miss Mink had been right on Main Street, handy to stores. As poor relation and professional doormat, she probably didn't have much of a wardrobe. Spot remover would be a useful thing to keep among her effects. After she'd got to the Bugginses', she might have kept the bottle hidden for fear Beatrice would use it up on her or Trevelyan would get to wondering if the stuff was fit to drink.

People had been known to commit murders for petty reasons, especially toward the end of a long, bleak winter when the cabin fever got to them and the weather was raising hell with their sciatica and they still had to go on boiling the porridge every morning. Miss Mink could even have stuck the ice pick into that stranger's neck when he dropped in to see his long-lost relatives, assuming they were and he had.

Shandy knew he mustn't assume all three deaths were

related until he'd found some proof that they were, but why waste time thinking they weren't? If Miss Mink had stabbed the stranger, though, it would seem she must have done so out at First Fork. So how in the flaming blue blazes had a woman her age, plagued with a game leg, pedaled a corpse his size all the way to Oozak's Pond sometime in January on the back of a bicycle? Shandy gave up thinking and concentrated on the road.

Seven Forks was becoming gentrified, he noticed as they got past the town dump. Time was when you couldn't have told which was town and which was dump out here. However, since Captain Amos Flackley had come home from Antarctica to take over the family farriery at Forgery Point, he'd been hectoring his neighbors to pen up their hens and pigs, clear away the junk cluttering their dooryards, and nail back the clapboards on their houses.

Flackley had started a kind of cooperative do-it-yourself shop, enabling residents to buy paint and other needed materials at cost, on the installment plan if necessary. His wife, Yvette, was running sewing and upholstery classes and planning a neighborhood landscaping project for when the weather got warm enough. Where erst the locals' idea of haute cuisine had been a sixpack of Bud and a take-out pizza, one now heard rumors of fondue pots and wine tastings. Shandy went back to thinking.

"Ottermole, how much of First Fork did Trevelyan Buggins own?"

"Huh? Oh, I dunno. Most of it, I guess. None of it worth a hoot."

And taxed accordingly, otherwise Buggins couldn't have held on to it all these years. And the only reason he had kept the land was that he hadn't been able to find a sucker to unload it on, no doubt.

"By George!" he exclaimed.

"Huh?" said Ottermole again.

"Sorry. I was just thinking. Why do you say First Fork

isn't worth a hoot? Kindly reflect, Ottermole, that the Seven Forks lie closer to the county seat than any other large tract of land that isn't being farmed or built on. Most of the owners are as hard up as the Bugginses were and would no doubt sell out like a shot if some developer made them an offer. Look what's happened over in Lumpkinton, with that pirate Gunnar Gaffson slapping up his cracker-box condominiums right and left."

"Jeez, I never thought of that. D'you suppose that's why Captain Flackley's gettin' everybody to fix up their property?"

"I'd rather think he's just trying to help them to a better way of life. Of course, he may see the possibility of a takeover and figure that if the owners spruce up their places, they can attract individual buyers and keep some control over the neighborhood instead of letting some big developer rip the whole place apart to suit himself."

"Huh," said Ottermole, in whom the viewing of many cops-and-robbers movies had planted the seeds of cynicism, "or Flackley himself aims to buy the houses cheap and sell 'em high once the owners have got 'em looking good. He could do it through a phony real-estate trust, an' they'd never know it was him."

"M'yes, I daresay he could."

Easy as falling off a log. Shandy didn't like this notion one bit. He'd admired the scientist-explorer who'd given up a thrilling career in the Antarctic and settled down to maintain a family tradition. But what if Flackley had acted not out of concern for the unshod hooves of Balaclava County horses but from the realization that here lay a chance to enrich himself at his unwary neighbors' expense and go back to exploring without having to scrounge for any more grants?

What if the farrier had already approached Trevelyan Buggins about selling off his large holdings? What if the old man had told him to get lost on the grounds that he himself was about to get rich and preferred to keep the ancestral acres intact for future generations? What if Flackley had pressed Buggins to reconsider, and what if old Trevelyan had sent for his son to help him withstand Flackley's badgering? What if Bracebridge, or possibly Bainbridge, had got tough, and what if the farrier had got tougher?

Shandy didn't know how hot tempers had been wont to flare in the southernmost latitudes, but he did know a fair amount about Captain Amos Flackley. Royall Ames, son of Shandy's close friend Professor Timothy Ames, had met his wife, Laurie, while both were serving as biologists aboard Flackley's ship, the *Hippocampus*. The captain had actually presided at their wedding, attended by the ship's crew and several hundred penguins.

According to Roy and Laurie, Captain Flackley was a man of infinite resource and indomitable courage. He was no reckless ice rover who rushed in where others feared to mush, but neither had they ever seen him flinch from any dauntless deed of derring-do that needed to be done. Should Captain Flackley decide Bracebridge Buggins or his reasonable facsimile ought to be stabbed in the neck and shoved into Oozak's Pond dressed in a funny suit with rocks in the pockets, then Captain Flackley would no doubt accomplish the task with a minimum of fuss and get on to the next thing. As for the ice pick, what more appropriate weapon for a man who'd spent so many years among the bergs and floes?

Oozak's Pond wasn't the Weddell Sea, but it was a darned sight closer. Flackley would know the pond never froze over. If he didn't recall that fact from his boyhood, he could easily have picked it up when he made his bi-weekly visit to shoe Thorkjeld Svenson's Balaclava Blacks or exchange sage words with Professor Stott about the care and feeding of hogs, sheep, and elephant seals. Stott had no elephant seals under his care at the moment, but one never knew.

Perdition! Flackley had the brains and the enterprise, he had at least a hypothetical motive, and he was right here on the spot. What more likely suspect could a person want?

What Peter Shandy wanted was somebody he didn't like. He was in an even more somber mood than he'd started out with by the time they reached the Buggins place. Miss Mink had been here alone when Edna Mae Ottermole had telephoned awhile back at her husband's guileful hest, ostensibly to see how she was feeling. By now, the woman could have been joined by an assortment of Minks and Porbles or taken away to one of their homes.

No, by George, she was still here and still alone. She hadn't been for long, though, unless she indulged in the long-ago country woman's habit of smoking a pipe. When she opened the door, the unmistakable smell hung in the air, overpowering various other odors of old house and stale cooking. Her greeting was unenthusiastic.

"Oh, it's you."

"Had lots of company, Miss Mink?" Shandy asked her.

She sniffed. "If you can call it that. Nosy neighbors coming to snoop would be nearer the mark. But it was either stay here and put up with their impertinence or go to Persephone's and listen to Purvis's mother simper and sigh. Grace Porble did offer me a bed, but I knew better than to take her up on it. Dr. Porble's far too high and mighty to be bothered with the likes of me."

Phil Porble would hardly have turned an old woman out in the snow. Miss Mink must know that. She must also know that Persephone would let her stay here until she found another place, however long that might be. Shandy wondered whether Miss Mink might be scheming to acquire the house for herself on the basis of squatter's rights.

Ottermole produced a small jar from one of the many pockets in his black leather jacket. "Here, Miss Mink. My wife sent you some preserves."

Edna Mae had done her gift up nicely. A circle of pinked gingham was tied over the lid with a red ribbon and a sprig of dried statice tucked under it like a flower in a hatband. They were going to love Edna Mae at the garden club. Miss Mink set the jar on the table with a weary sigh.

"I'll drop her a note when I get the chance."

"You don't have to bother."

"I know my duty, Frederick Ottermole. Why do you suppose they always send strawberry?"

Shandy decided now was as good a time as any to give this unpleasant old person the raspberry. "Miss Mink," he said, "have you been in touch with Persephone anytime during the past few hours?"

"What do you mean by the past few hours? Sephy was out here this morning to pick up the clothes for her parents to be laid out in. You saw her yourself. She phoned again about half past three to say it was all set about the funeral and ask if I wanted to go in town and stay with her and Purvis tonight. I did not. I reminded her that somebody had better stay here and hold the fort or certain people I shan't dignify by naming would be in here stealing everything they could lay their filthy hands on."

"Then you haven't heard the final verdict on Mr. and Mrs. Buggins?"

"What verdict? Dr. Fotheringay signed the death certificate."

"Nope," said Ottermole. "That hot-dog pen you loaned him run dry before he finished writing his name. He just kept scratchin' away without noticing the ink wasn't coming out."

"That still counts as signing."

"Not to me it don't. He should o' known better, anyways.

Doctors aren't supposed to sign death certificates in suspicious circumstances."

"The circumstances were hardly suspicious. Both Mr. and Mrs. Buggins had been ailing all winter."

"Not the way they ailed last night. Hey, you better sit down here in the rocking chair, Miss Mink."

"Why should I?"

She was, after all, an old woman. "Because," said Shandy, "we have some shocking news for you. Sit down, Miss Mink."

Chapter 9

Shandy moved the rocking chair closer to the wood stove. After some flouncing and grumbling, Miss Mink allowed him to seat her.

"All right, what is it? After what I've been through today, I don't suppose anything could faze me much."

Shandy gave up trying to be tactful. "The autopsy showed both Mr. and Mrs. Buggins had been poisoned."

"Autopsy? What right had anybody to—" She must have realized it was too late to argue. "What kind of poison?"

"Carbon tetrachloride."

She stared at him. "You're trying to trick me, aren't you? I know what that means, and I say it's ridiculous. Don't you think the Bugginses would have had more sense than to drink cleaning fluid? They weren't senile, you know."

"We're not trying to trick you, Miss Mink. Did you have any in the house?"

"Of course not. What would we want it for? Anything her parents needed to have cleaned Persephone took over to the Sunny Spot."

"Then we're left with the assumption that somebody brought the poison here."

"Not me."

"I'm not saying it was you, Miss Mink. Chief Ottermole and I are only trying to find out who it might have been. We hope you'll be able to help us."

"I can't." All at once, Miss Mink's brass-plated composure had developed a serious crack. "I wasn't here. I deserted my post. I failed them in their time of need. Oh, Lord, forgive me! Why wasn't I taken instead?"

She flung her apron up over her face and started rocking frantically. The rocker scooted backward over the uneven wide-board floor. Shandy had to leap aside or be rocked over.

"Ottermole, is there any hot water in that kettle? Miss Mink could use a cup of tea to steady her nerves."

"I don't deserve any tea," Miss Mink moaned from under her apron. "I'm a wicked sinner."

"Aw, heck," said Ottermole, "it ain't that bad. Here, take a swallow of this."

The housekeeper rubbed viciously at her face with the apron, let it fall, and glared at the sloppy mug Ottermole was holding out to her with the teabag's little cardboard tag floating on top. "How am I to know it isn't poisoned?"

"What do you care?" the chief retorted. "You just said why wasn't it you instead of them? Anyway, how could carbon tetrachloride get into a teabag?"

"It might be in the water."

"No chance. The water was boiling. Carbon tet would o' turned into phosgene gas an' leaked out the spout."

"Good gad, Ottermole, I didn't know that," said Shandy. "Where did you pick up such esoteric knowledge?"

"I called up Professor Joad in the chemistry department. See, I figured they'd keep a kettle boilin' on the wood stove, so I thought I'd better check it out." There were, as Edna Mae had been trying for years to convince her relatives, no flies on Fred Ottermole.

Thus reassured, Miss Mink essayed a sip of the tea. "Humph," she complained, "you might have put a little milk and sugar in it."

Meekly, Chief Ottermole fetched the sugar bowl off the kitchen table and the milk from the circa 1954 Frigidaire. The larder was well stocked, Shandy noticed. Probably Grace and Persephone had brought groceries with them.

He waited until Miss Mink had got her tea doctored to her liking and downed about half the mugful, then risked another question.

"Would you mind telling us where you went last night?"

Miss Mink finished her tea, carried the mug to the sink, rinsed it under the faucet, set it in the dish drainer to dry, walked back, and sat down in the rocking chair with her face turned toward the stove. "I was at the bingo," she muttered.

"Thus do our sins find us out," Shandy murmured. "Ah yes, the bingo. Where was it being held, Miss Mink?"

"Over at Fourth Fork."

"They got a kind of community hall over there," Ottermole explained to Shandy. "It used to be a schoolhouse till they started busin' the kids over to the center. "How'd you get there, Miss Mink?"

"I was driven."

"Who by?"

"One of the neighbors." She flapped her apron as if she were trying to shoo her bothersome visitors away. "Well, I have to get out of here sometimes, don't I? Cooped up in this poky house day after day, night after night, waiting on the pair of them hand and foot with never a letup."

"Aw, come on, Min. You had them Bugginses right where you wanted 'em. An' don't think we all didn't know it."

The speaker was the lady in red, blowing in out of the night, her hair a shade frowsier, her general aspect if possible more bedraggled. Instead of the windbreaker, she had on a fake-fur coat. Imitation wombat, Shandy thought. He wondered if she'd salvaged the garment from some long-distance truck driver who'd been in the habit of using it to wipe the stains of travel off his sixteen-wheeler.

"I didn't hear you knock" was Miss Mink's icy greeting.

"The door was open."

"It was not."

"Okay, then, but it wasn't latched tight. I brung you a bunch o' magazines to while away the time. Don't I even rate a thanks?"

"I have no time to fritter away on your kind of reading matter."

"Still sore 'cause you didn't win last night, eh?"

Shandy intervened. "You were also at the bingo last night, Miss, er?"

"Just call me Flo. You married?"

"Very happily, thank you."

"Well, any time." Flo didn't put much enthusiasm into her invitation, if such it was. "What's up?"

"We are having a private discussion." Miss Mink was probably too refined to snarl, but she came pretty close.

"Get her," said Flo. "She's still mad as hell 'cause I wouldn't stay for the last game."

"How late was this, er, Flo?" Shandy asked her.

"I dunno. Eleven o'clock, ha' past, maybe. Min don't ever want to leave till the last gun's fired an' the smoke's cleared away. Me, I gotta get my beauty sleep. Anybody spare a cigarette?"

Nobody could. Edna Mae had made Ottermole quit smoking because he was setting a bad example to his sons. Shandy had been too poor to afford bad habits back when he'd been callow enough to have acquired them. Miss Mink only sniffed. Flo didn't look as if she'd expected to be given one, anyway. Shandy noticed she hadn't even bothered to remove the red knitted gloves she was wearing. In contrast to the rest of her garb, they looked new and clean. Maybe she'd just bought them out of her bingo winnings and wanted to show them off.

"Was it you who drove Miss Mink to the hall?" Shandy asked her.

"That's right. I got my friend's car. He's away." Flo glared at Chief Ottermole.

"Oh, yeah?" he replied with understandable interest. "What did they get him on?"

This, Shandy felt, was hardly the time for professional chitchat. "What time did you pick Miss Mink up, do you know that?"

"Right after *Doctor Who*. Maybe twenty minutes to eight."

"Did you see Mr. and Mrs. Buggins at that time? Were they all right?"

"Sure. They come flappin' an' squawkin' like a pair of old hens, same as always, wantin' me to come in an' set a spell. But Min here had her coat an' hat all on, an' I knew she was champin' at the bit to get goin', so I says we didn't want to miss the first game an' we went. You get free coffee if you go early, see."

"You didn't expect the Bugginses to be sitting up for you when you got back, Miss Mink?"

"Oh, no, never. They went to bed every night at half past nine on the dot."

"Didn't have much to sit up for," Flo put in.

Shandy turned to her. "Did you come to the house with Miss Mink when you dropped her off after the bingo?"

"Hell, no. I was scared I'd wake up ol' Pop Buggins. Then he'd come down an' I'd have to listen to him tellin' them same ol' yarns without his teeth in. They was bad enough when you could understand what he was sayin', but when he talked like a bowlful o' Wheatena, forget it. I just sat there with the motor runnin' till Min got inside, then scrammed."

"Miss Mink, did you happen to look in on Mr. and Mrs. Buggins before you went to bed?"

"I am not in the habit of bursting into the bedrooms of married couples without their express permission," Miss Mink replied in a tone of chilling reproof.

"Gawd, ain't she got class," cried Flo. "Too bad she's come down to bummin' rides offa the likes o' me. Well, see you around, fellas. I gotta go. They're havin' a *Gilligan's Island* festival on."

"It ain't till tomorrow night," said Chief Ottermole, but Flo was already gone.

"Where does she live?" Shandy asked.

"In that blue cottage just as you turn off the county road," Miss Mink told him. "The regular occupant is, as she puts it, away."

"Mike Woozle," exclaimed Ottermole. "I knew it would come to me. Mike got eight to ten for robbin' the Petrolatorium over to Lumpkin Upper Mills."

"Wasn't that rather a stiff sentence for holding up a filling station?" Shandy asked.

"Yeah, but this was the fourteenth time he'd hit it. Besides, it was what you might call a special case. What happened was, Mike was givin' the boot to the Coke machine, tryin' to get the money out. Oscar Plantagenet, the guy that owns the station, lives right next door, see. Oscar hears Mike kickin' the machine, so he grabs his kid's BB gun, that bein' the only weapon handy, an' runs over. Mike's got the Coke machine busted wide open by then, so he picks up a can of orangeade an' throws it at Oscar just as Oscar's tryin' to get a bead on Mike. So the BB gun goes off an' Oscar pings Mike in the left shin. So Mike gets sore. He's grabbin' cans of tonic an' chuckin' them at Oscar while Oscar's down behind the air pump tryin' to hit Mike's pitchin' arm with another BB. So then a bunch o' guys from the soap factory on the night shift happen along. They're all pals of Oscar's, so they start pickin' up the cans an' throwin' them back at Mike."

"Gad, a veritable Armageddon."

"You can say that again. Mike's got a hunk of the Coke machine he's usin' for a shield like them Roman gladiators, an' he's lammin' the cans back an' Oscar's shootin' them down in midair with the BB gun. There's Seven-Up an' ginger ale squirtin' all over the place 'cause the carbonation's stirred up from the chuckin' around. It's like hell broke loose out there.

"So by this time, Oscar's wife's called the police. Chief Olson comes chargin' over an' Mike wings him on the right ear with a can o' root beer. Mike's standin' there crackin' up at Olson wipin' the root beer off his face an' one of the guys from the soap factory that's into martial arts sneaks up behind Mike like that guy in *Kung Fu* an' yells 'Ha-ya' an' kicks Mike's feet out from under him.

"So then six or eight o' the guys from the soap factory pile on top of Mike. By then, Olson's got the root beer out of his eyes an' remembered where he put his handcuffs, so he makes the collar, only he has to heave a couple o' the guys off the pile first so's he can get at Mike's wrist. So the judge charges Mike with robbery with violence an' criminal assault with twenty-six cans of carbonated beverages."

"And thus was a new page written in the annals of justice," said Shandy. "Damned shame Oscar's wife didn't take movies. How long has this, er, Flo been consorting with Mike Woozle, Miss Mink?"

The woman shrugged. "I wouldn't know. He's always had floozies coming and going. As a rule, they leave me alone and I do the same, but lately this one's been hanging around trying to be friendly, if you can call it that. I expect she's lonesome since that Woozle man went to jail, and doesn't know what else to do with herself. I've tried to make it plain I don't much care for her company, but Flo isn't one to take a hint."

"Must be handy, havin' somebody around to give you a lift, though," said Ottermole.

Miss Mink had to concede that it was. "But when I think of myself sitting over there playing bingo while Mr. and Mrs. Buggins were in their last extremities—oh, I can't bear it! Do you think I could have saved them if I'd been here?"

"M'well, that's a moot point," said Shandy. "I under-

stand it was their mutual custom to take a glassful of Mr.
Buggins's special blend before they went to bed."

"That's right. Not a large glassful, you know. It was just
to help them sleep."

"If you'd been here last night, would you have had one
with them?"

"I suppose so," Miss Mink admitted, "if they'd offered it
to me."

"Would they have been apt to do so?"

"Like as not. The Bugginses weren't stingy, like some
I've known."

"But you wouldn't have helped yourself without being
asked."

"Oh, no, never. I wouldn't dream of such a thing."

Miss Mink stared at him. "Good heavens! Are you
implying that if I hadn't been away last night, I'd be dead
now myself?"

"The possibility has to be considered, Miss Mink,"
Shandy replied.

"Want some more tea?" said Ottermole.

She shied as if he'd tried to bean her with a can of root
beer. "Heavens, no! I couldn't touch a thing. You might
put another stick of wood on the fire if you want to be
helpful. I feel chilly all of a sudden."

Miss Mink hugged the gray worsted cardigan around
her. "Maybe it would have been wiser to go to Persephone's
after all."

"We'll be glad to run you over," Shandy offered, but she
shook her head.

"No, I told them I'd stay, and I'm not going back on my
word. After all, what does it matter, an old woman like me?
The Bugginses surely don't need me anymore."

She laughed a bit crazily. Shandy hoped she wasn't
working herself up for another outburst.

"You just sit there and warm yourself, Miss Mink. Chief

Ottermole's going to take a look around and make sure there's nothing in the house that could harm you."

"Yeah," said Ottermole. "Like where's that jug o' booze they drank out of?"

"In that left-hand corner cupboard beside the sink. The label says vinegar. Mr. Buggins simply used whatever receptacles came to hand."

"That's how come you got so much vinegar here, eh?" The chief had his head in the cupboard. "Here's a jug half empty, so it must be the one they poured from. Give a sniff, Professor."

"Thanks," said Shandy. "If there's carbon tetrachloride in it, I'd rather not and neither should you. We'll take the jug along to Professor Joad and let him run a test. Miss Mink, during the time you were out of the house, would the Bugginses have kept the doors locked?"

"Who, them? That pair never locked a door in their lives. Nobody did out here when they were growing up, and they couldn't be made to see any need for it these days. They'd have left the door unlocked for me in any case, I expect. People don't care to trust their hired help with their keys, do they? Assuming they happened to remember where the keys were."

Shandy ignored the dig. "And would the Bugginses have been sitting here by the stove?"

"They weren't when I left. Their television set's upstairs. After Persephone moved out, Mr. Buggins fixed her bedroom over into what he liked to call his den. Usually, they'd go straight up there after supper. While I washed the dishes and straightened up the kitchen," she added with one of her sniffs.

"Is the den heated?"

"Oh, yes, it's warm enough. The chimney goes up through, and there's a register cut in the floor. Besides, he and she both had those comforter things you stick your feet inside and zip up around you."

"And that's how you left them?"

"To the best of my knowledge, yes. We'd had supper at six, as usual, then they went up to watch the news, and that's the last I saw of them till Flo stopped by to pick me up. They came down then, as she said, but once they realized she wasn't going to stay, they went back upstairs. There was some program they wanted to watch."

"Their bedroom is also upstairs, I believe?" Shandy remembered Miss Mink had gone up there to fetch the anniversary photograph that morning.

"And the bathroom," she amplified.

"You didn't, er, have occasion to visit the facilities before you yourself went to bed last night?"

"I did not. Purvis installed a makeshift sink and commode in what used to be the summer kitchen. I use that mostly."

"And where do you sleep?"

"In the hired hand's room off the kitchen, naturally."

"May we see?"

Miss Mink buttoned her lips extremely tight but did not resist. Shandy couldn't see how she had much to complain about in her quarters. There was a comfortable-looking single iron bed with a white candlewick spread and a fancy knitted afghan folded over the foot. She'd been given an upholstered armchair and a chest of drawers on which stood her own small television set. A nightstand held a reading lamp, a clock radio, a Bible prominently displayed, and a couple of paperback bodice rippers half hidden behind it. Sentimental chromos hung on the walls, blue nylon curtains at the windows. Braided rugs covered the floor, and enough gewgaws sat around to start a gift shop.

"Very cozy," he remarked to Miss Mink's evident displeasure. "We'll just check around a bit, if you don't mind."

"What difference does it make whether I mind or not?" Miss Mink snapped back. "You'll do it anyway."

That was true enough, so they did. Their search was both distasteful and fruitless, her only guilty secret being a stack of magazines she insisted Flo had forced on her and she'd been too embarrassed to put in the trash for Purvis to haul to the dump. They were relieved to get back to the kitchen.

"What about those drinks?" Shandy asked her. "Did the Bugginses take them upstairs right after supper?"

"Oh, no, never. One or the other would come down to get them while they were getting ready for bed. They were both spry enough when they wanted to be."

"Then it looks to me as if anybody who took the notion could have walked into the house and put poison in the jug any time between a quarter of eight and half past nine. Is that your theory, Miss Mink?"

"I didn't realize it was my place to have a theory." She must be still miffed about the magazines. "But I don't see how else it could have happened. Mr. Buggins had had a couple during the day, and he was still alive and kicking at suppertime, so the liquor must have been all right up till then. The Bugginses wouldn't have heard anybody come in while they were upstairs. They kept that television blaring a good deal too loud for my liking, I don't mind telling you."

"The intruder would have had to know where the Bugginses kept their liquor, though," said Shandy. "Wouldn't that vinegar jug have put anybody off?"

Miss Mink sniffed. "Not so you'd notice it. I've heard enough about Trev Buggins and his vinegar jugs over at bingo. He used to pick them up at the town dump during pickling time. Not to speak disrespectfully of my late employer, that still of his has been a standing joke around the Seven Forks ever since I've been here and a long time before that. I daresay somebody's sneaked in and helped himself to a swig of Mr. Buggins's whiskey now and then, but I don't know that anyone's ever tried to poison it before. From the cracks they make, they all think it's rank poison already."

"But nobody ever died from drinkin' it till now," Ottermole pointed out. "Not unless you count D.T.'s or hobnail liver."

"I wouldn't know about such things," said Miss Mink, contriving to make them sound like nasty things indeed, "though I expect they're common enough around these parts. It's a class of people I'm not accustomed to associating with, I don't mind telling you, but I suppose beggars can't be choosers. If you've finished poking through my personal belongings, do you think it might be possible to leave me in peace? I'd been hoping I might get a decent night's sleep for a change."

"And I hope you do, Miss Mink," Shandy replied courteously. "One more question, please, and then we'll go. Did anybody at all come to the house yesterday other than your, er, neighbor?"

"Why, yes, now that you mention it. None other than the great Dr. Porble in person."

"And what did Dr. Porble come for?"

"To pick a fight over the lawsuit, naturally. Which, I must say, he did in grand style. I thought he was going to tear this house apart with his bare hands before he got through. You'd never believe a man who prides himself so much on his dignity could turn into a raving maniac all of a sudden, would you?"

Chapter 10

"No," said Shandy, "I'd never believe it."

"Meaning I'm a liar, I suppose. Well, you can just go and ask—" She caught her breath.

"Ask whom, Miss Mink?"

"I was going to say ask Mrs. Buggins. But she's gone, isn't she?" The housekeeper's voice had become awfully gentle all of a sudden.

"Come on, Professor," muttered Ottermole, "I think we better go. You get some sleep, Miss Mink. You'll feel better in the morning."

She didn't answer, merely went to the door and held it open. After they'd gone out, they could hear her shooting the bolt.

"Anyways, she's got sense enough left to bolt the door," Ottermole remarked as they got into the car.

"I was a damned fool to push her like that," said Shandy. "I should have remembered what a hell of a day she's had. I hope we didn't make a mistake leaving her here alone."

"Ah, she's a tough old bird. I bet she's havin' herself a slug o' Trev's oh-be-joyful right now."

"If she can do that, she's tough enough for anything and I shan't feel like such a rat. At least she'll have to open a fresh bottle. I can't imagine whoever it was bothered to poison the whole batch."

"We'll know in the morning," Ottermole replied through a jaw-splitting yawn. "You really think she was puttin' us on about Dr. Porble?"

"I'm inclined to think she engaged in hyperbole."

"Huh?"

"Exaggerating the truth for rhetorical effect. She tends to do that, I've noticed."

"Oh, yeah, like when she was talkin' about grindin' the faces of the poor this morning. What the hell, I'm none too flush myself, but if some rich guy waltzed up to me an' said, 'I'm gonna grind your face,' I'd damn well tell 'im where to head in. So would she, for all her mealymouth bitchin'. Where to now, Professor? Home, I hope?"

"I hope so, too, Ottermole. But first, since the night is still relatively young and since we're in the neighborhood, I was thinking we ought to pay a call on Captain Flackley."

"What for? We ain't goin' to pinch him, are we?"

"Not tonight, as far as I know. It occurred to me that it might be a good idea for some responsible neighbor to know Miss Mink is alone in the Buggins house."

Then again, if it had been Flackley who murdered the Bugginses, it might be a spectacularly bad idea. Shandy couldn't see any reason why the farrier would want to come back and kill the housekeeper, though. The fact that whoever spiked the vinegar jug picked a night when Miss Mink would be out playing bingo could be an indication that she wasn't meant to die with the others, though it was more likely a matter of her absence making access to the jug a lot simpler. Anyway, if Flackley was in fact playing a double game, it would be more in keeping with his role to show the lone survivor every consideration.

Shandy knew Forgery Point well enough. The old Flackley place was out at the end of Second Fork. Getting there by road meant doubling back to where the Seven Forks met and submitting his car to another longish stretch of ruts and bumps. Cutting through the woods would be far shorter and a cinch for a man who was not only used to skis and snowshoes but even had his own team of huskies.

Dogsled racing had begun to catch on in Balaclava

County. Captain Flackley had naturally been pleased to find out that the hardy canines who'd been with him aboard the *Hippocampus* would be, if not quite welcome, at least tolerated around Forgery Point. Roy and Laurie Ames would have liked a team, too, but public opinion at the Crescent, including the Shandys' and Jane Austen's, was against them.

One thing about huskies, though, they saved visitors' having to hunt for a probably nonexistent doorbell in the dark. Shandy and Ottermole weren't out of the car before a chorus of "Awoo" in eight different tones rent the air. The huskies were penned up behind a chain-link fence, but even so, the wolflike howls were somewhat unnerving.

Flackley himself opened the front door, bellowed "Shut up," at which command all eight huskies miraculously did, and managed to tell his visitors that this was an unexpected pleasure without making it too obvious that while he was clear about the unexpected, he had his doubts with regard to the pleasure.

"Come in, come in. Don't fret about your boots, this floor's fairly slushproof. What can I get you? Yvette's at her rug-making class, but I brew a great cup of instant coffee."

"Thanks, but we weren't intending to stay," Shandy told him. "We're on our way back to the Junction. We only stopped to speak to you about Miss Mink over at First Fork. I expect you've heard about the Bugginses?"

"Lord, yes, every place I worked today, I got an earful. The only ones who didn't talk about it were the horses. Both husband and wife dying the same night and that poor old soul finding them all by herself. Must have taken an awful hike out of her."

Captain Flackley was a big man, even bigger than Fred Ottermole, though, of course, nowhere near the size of President Svenson. His hair was the color of frost but didn't make him look old. His face was ruddy, his brown eyes snapped, his well-muscled frame suggested vigorous motion even when he was sitting perfectly still. He could have passed for thirty-five or so, but Shandy knew he had two sons old enough to have assumed his work aboard the *Hippocampus* and a daughter studying animal husbandry with Professor Stott and farriery with her father.

"Sit down," Flackley urged. "You can stop a minute. I was just going over some figures, and all interruptions are welcome. That's one job I hate, but it has to be done. Now what's this about Miss Mink?"

"Simply that she's got nobody with her and is in, er, considerable distress of mind."

"Because the Bugginses were murdered?"

He hadn't lost any time getting to the point. "So you've heard about that, too?" Shandy said.

"At least seventeen different versions. What happened? Were they stabbed, smothered, strangled with Mrs. Buggins's corset strings, or poisoned by Trevelyan's booze?"

"Actually, it was the booze."

"You're kidding! Good God, I've got a jug of the stuff right here in the house. Haven't got up nerve enough to sample it myself yet, but I tried half a pint on a mare with a case of glanders the vet couldn't seem to get rid of. Straightened her out fine as silk in three days. I told Buggins he ought to take out a patent, but he couldn't remember what that particular batch was made of."

"This must have been a different batch."

Shandy decided he might as well tell Flackley the whole story. It would be all over the county by morning, anyway. "What we think happened was that somebody poured poison into an already opened jug, which naturally would have been the one Mr. and Mrs. Buggins took their usual bedtime drink from. Miss Mink didn't drink any with them because she'd gone out to play bingo."

"What was the poison?"

"Carbon tetrachloride."

"I'll be darned." Flackley shook his head. "That's one I'd

never have thought of. Not a bad choice, though, I guess, if your mind was running that way. Hell, we've still got half a bottle sitting out in the woodshed because we can't think how best to get rid of it. Toxic waste, you know. My aunt must have kept it to clean her gloves with or something. God rest her soul, she was a fine woman and a damned good farrier but no chemist. You want to impound the bottle for evidence?"

"Maybe we better go take a look at it, anyways," said Ottermole.

Shandy didn't see why. Flackley's armchair was comfortable, Flackley's fire was bright. He himself would have been content to sit and rest awhile, but he didn't want to stifle the chief's initiative, so he went.

The Flackleys were tidy people, he noticed as they walked through the back entry to the woodshed. People who lived aboard ship learned to be, he supposed. The shed was new since Miss Flackley's time, though it probably replaced an earlier one that had been connected with the smithy. One side was hung with gardening implements, a dogsled harness, hand looms, upholstery stretchers, and other evidences of the family's multifarious interests. The other side was lined with shelves, all stacked with neatly labeled boxes, bins, cans, and jars. Flackley glanced along the top shelves, reached up, and took down a somewhat rusty coffee can.

"I stuck the bottle inside this, for fear some neighbor's kid might—" He shook the tin. "That's funny, there's nothing in it." He took off the lid and peered inside to make sure. "Nope, it's gone."

"Who took it?" Ottermole asked.

"My wife or daughter are the only ones I can think of offhand. They might have heard about a toxic waste collection drive somewhere, or one of Yvette's students got a bad stain on the piece he'd been upholstering—I don't know."

He slammed the lid down on the can and set it back on the shelf. "I'll ask her when she gets home. No sense getting all worked up till we find out whether there's anything to panic about."

"None whatever," Shandy agreed. "What time is Mrs. Flackley due back?"

"That's hard to say. The class is supposed to be over at half past nine, but they get interested, you know, and then there's the mess to clean up afterward. We can go over to the community hall and ask her if you think it's important."

And start every tongue in the place wagging at full speed? Shandy shook his head. "It can wait. Do you recall when you last saw the bottle yourself?"

"Gosh, I'm not sure. Let's see. We had a red squirrel and his wife—at least I assume she was his wife—get in here last fall and try to set up housekeeping. They were running along the shelves, knocking things down and making a mess. This can was one of the things they kicked off, I know. I definitely remember looking inside to make sure they hadn't broken the bottle because I didn't want the fumes leaking out. It was all right, so I put the can back up there, which was stupid of me. I should have taken care of it then and there, but all I could think of were those pesky squirrels. You know what a job they can do on a place if you once let them get a toehold."

Ottermole started a tale of woe about squirrels in his own attic, but Shandy headed him off. "Was anybody with you at the time?"

"Why, yes, a fellow named Zack Woozle who helps us around the place quite a lot. He saw me open the can and made some crack about 'What you got in there, Cap'n? A jar of Buggins's booze?' So I thought I'd better explain what was in the bottle and why I'd hidden it away so Zack wouldn't be tempted to try a snort."

"Zack Woozle?" said Ottermole. "Isn't he a brother or

cousin or somethin' of the Mike Woozle that held up the gas station over at Lumpkin Upper Mills?"

"I expect so," Flackley replied. "There are a good many Woozles around the Seven Forks, and chances are they're all connected one way or another. Zack's okay. Most of them are, and there's nothing much wrong with the rest except poverty and lack of effective training, as far as Yvette and I can see."

"Is Zack Woozle married?" Shandy asked.

"Yes. His wife's a nice woman. Rather dressy."

"Does she play bingo?"

The farrier blinked, then smiled. "I see what you're getting at. Sure, I daresay she and Zack both do. Bingo's the big thing around here, you know. They play for a dime a card, something like that. Silly waste of time, to my way of thinking, but I can't see any real harm in it. At least it's sociability of a sort. And, yes, I shouldn't be surprised if Zack was joking at the hall about thinking I had a bottle of liquor hidden in the woodshed and it turned out to be carbon tetrachloride."

"Do you keep the woodshed locked?"

"Not during the daytime and seldom at night, if you want the truth. There's the forge, you know, and we're always needing one thing or another out of the shed. Anybody could have come in and taken it, if he'd a mind to. Maybe some kid, thinking he'd get high by sniffing the bottle, poor little jackass. Or maybe some grown-up with a grudge against the Bugginses. Damn, I wish I'd poured the stuff out on the ground and been done with it. That's what comes of having principles."

"Nobody's going to fault you for not wanting to pollute the environment," Shandy assured him. "We can't know for sure that yours was the carbon tetrachloride that killed the Bugginses. If it was, you can console yourself with the thought that if it hadn't been handy, they could easily enough have found something else."

"That doesn't excuse my carelessness," said Flackley. "I'm afraid I haven't been much help to you."

Shandy was afraid not, too. Much as he'd have preferred to take the explorer at face value, he didn't feel encouraged to do so. Naturally Captain Flackley had had to admit there'd been carbon tetrachloride on the place if his hired man had gone snickering about it to his bingo buddies. Keeping a toxic substance inside a rusty coffee can didn't strike Professor Shandy as a particularly intelligent solution to what had, after all, been an insignificant problem. Granted, it was the sort of thing any householder might do, but Amos Flackley wasn't just anybody.

Unless the farrier had kept the bottle as a subconscious act of piety toward his late aunt's memory. The premise was a doubtful one at best. Shandy was not happy as he slid back behind the steering wheel.

Chief Ottermole wasn't happy, either. He'd begun chewing gum with what might have been perhaps overdramatically described as savage intensity, blowing little bubbles and popping them back as if he hated them. Shandy turned on the car radio hoping to drown out the pops, but Ottermole only began puffing and snapping in time with the music.

This unceasing spearmint roulade might perhaps have been inspirational to a composer. To a middle-aged professor who'd had a long, bad day, it was next to unendurable. He was to no end relieved when at last he dropped his eruptive passenger off at the blue house with the white shutters, where Edna Mae was doubtless waiting with arms outstretched and ears atilt for the latest thrilling adventure in the ongoing saga of Fred Ottermole, Supercop.

Helen was waiting, too, in front of the living-room fire with Jane Austen curled up on her lap and a bundle of Bugginsana on the lamp table beside her. She'd been napping but woke when she heard Shandy's step and held up her face for a kiss.

"Hello, darling. How did you make out?"

He sighed and flopped down on the settee beside her. "Who knows? Miss Mink claims Phil Porble was out there yesterday throwing a tantrum over the lawsuit. She claims she was afraid he'd tear the place apart with his bare hands."

"Did you believe her?"

"In a word, no. She didn't take kindly to my dubiety."

"So then what did you do?"

"Folded my tents like the Arabs and as quietly snuck away. I think that allusion is a trifle outdated. So's Miss Mink. She was in fairly wan condition by then. As am I."

"Poor you. Would you like some hot cocoa? It's all made."

"Got any animal crackers to go with it?"

"Peter Shandy, if you start quoting *A Child's Garden of Verses* at me, I shall rush screaming out into the night and ruin my brand-new bedroom slippers. I've been reading Corydon Buggins's poetry until I quail at the mere thought of an iambic footfall."

"May one hope that you found something significant?"

"Would you settle for a red-hot love affair with a girl named Arbolene Woozle?"

"By thunder, Helen, I knew you could do it! Was this union, er, fructified?"

"I shouldn't be at all surprised. Corydon appears to have been going through what might be termed his Robbie Burns period at the time."

" 'I'll ne'er forget that happy night among the cornstalks wi' Arbolene.' Stuff like that?"

"Like that and a good deal more so. Imogene and he grew gracious wi' favors secret, sweet, and downright unprintable, even in Corydon's private notebook. I found one fragment that began, 'Arbolene, my lusty queen,

thou ———est like a gasogene.' As to what the ———
represented, I leave you to conjecture. I'm much too pure-
minded a lady myself. But surely there aren't any
Woozles?"

"Ah, but there are. One Woozle is even now languishing
in the county bastille for bopping Chief Olson of Lumpkinton with a can of root beer out of a vandalized vending
machine at the Gasoline Alley Petrolatorium. Another
Woozle does chores for Captain Flackley *et ux*. Out at the
Seven Forks, the woods are full of Woozles."

"Then I say Fred Ottermole had better go out there
tomorrow and find out whether they're short a Woozle.
Here, Jane, go to Papa while I get the cocoa. I'm afraid the
only animal crackers we have are Kitty Krumbles, dear.
Would you settle for gingersnaps?"

Chapter 11

S handy had classes the next morning. Before he left the house, though, he phoned Chief Ottermole and explained what Helen had turned up about Corydon and Arbolene. "So my wife thinks it would be an excellent move for you to go back out to Seven Forks and run a check on missing Woozles. That might help us identify the chap in Goulson's icebox."

Ottermole had just got to the station and settled down for his usual morning visit with Mrs. Lomax's cat Edmund. He spoke as if his mouth were full of jelly doughnut, which in fact it was. "Budge Dorkin's been bustin' his britches to do some detecting. Why don't I send him instead?"

Shandy said that was a great idea and went on to his classroom. He found his students restive, as students often were, but not usually in Professor Shandy's classes. While he endeavored to alert them to the secret, evil work of the nematode, they demanded to hear about the secret, evil work of the fiend who'd dumped a corpse into the midst of their Groundhog Day revels, and was it true the demised had been wearing Balaclava Buggins's Sunday suit?

Professor Shandy assured them that the sacred relic was safe in its glass case in the Buggins Room and that if they expected to pass his course, they'd better keep their minds on the nematode. Thenceforth they tried, but it was uphill work for them—and for him. Even as he described the pitiable plight of a tender young radish with a worm in its bosom, his thoughts were on that empty coffee can in Amos Flackley's woodshed.

He wondered whether Mrs. or Miss Flackley had managed to come up with an innocent explanation for the missing bottle. He wondered further if Ottermole had thought to tell Dorkin to check Miss Mink's alibi. He put no faith in Flo. She looked to him like the type who wouldn't hesitate to lie in what she thought was a good cause and would certainly do so in a bad one.

He pondered the question of whether Persephone had been lying, too, Was there any way he could extract the truth of the matter without getting Purve and all the security guards, not to mention Grace, Helen, and the whole garden club, down on him?

He even debated a humanitarian visit to the bedside of Cronkite Swope. The young reporter must be feeling like a radish attacked by a nematode, lying there with Vicks up his nose and a mustard plaster on his chest, knowing that a story of the first magnitude was breaking and Arabella Goulson was snaffling his byline.

Gripped by the Sophoclean implications of Swope's bronchitic epiphany, Professor Shandy was able to put such pathos into his delivery that he at last succeeded in capturing his students' full and undivided attention. Sweeping them on from spider mites to cutworms, he soared to dramatic heights that had every student scribbling in his or her notebook with the concentrated zeal of a locust attacking a turnip green. They left his classroom shaken and trembling but uplifted and fired with a new dedication to the biological control of insect pests. Shandy mopped his brow and asked himself, "Where do I go from here?"

Lunch was the obvious answer. Shandy no longer timed his faculty dining room visits so as to afford maximum probability of catching Helen there, as he'd been wont to do back when love was young and Helen Marsh not yet

Mrs. Shandy, but he still tended to pause at the doorway and cast a hopeful glance around for a curly-haired blonde with a few tiger-colored cat hairs clinging to her skirt. He was unlucky today. Helen was not there. Her boss was.

Dr. Porble sat alone at one of the smaller tables consuming Tuna Surprise with cold ferocity. Coldness and ferocity weren't the easiest emotions to combine, Shandy thought as he sat down without waiting to be invited, but Porble was managing capably. He paused only to give Shandy a curt nod, then went on champing tuna fish.

Shandy gave his own order to a hovering restaurant-management major and opened diplomatic negotiations. "Hi, Phil. What's up?"

"My gorge," said the librarian, rending a hard roll in twain. "I expect you know why."

"I do. Our esteemed president has, er, handed me the baby. Any hints as to its care and feeding will be gratefully received."

"That lawsuit's a damned swindle."

"I think so, too. Any idea who dreamed it up?"

"One of old Trevelyan's half-baked notions, I suppose. He'd been steeping his brains so long in that sheep-dip he used to brew that he must have started believing his own fairy tales. I must say, I'm surprised Persephone didn't squash him before he got out of hand. I've always had a certain amount of respect for Sephy's intelligence, until now."

"You've, er, seen a fair amount of the Minks over the years, I understand."

"Oh, yes. Sephy and my wife are related, you know. She and Purve stood up with us at our wedding as a matter of fact. We four used to double-date sometimes before we got married. We still get together on occasion. Purve and I generally open the trout season together."

Dry fly-fishing was the only subject outside his family

and his library for which Dr. Porble ever showed much real enthusiasm. "I'd been looking forward to it," he added rather wistfully.

"This lawsuit isn't going to cause a rift in the lute?"

"The lute's already rifted, I'm afraid. When I found out what that senile idiot was up to, I went out and told him to lay off."

"Was that all you told him?"

Porble shrugged one shoulder and gave his colleague a wry smile. "Aunt Minnehaha's been talking, has she? All right, I lost my temper and gave it to him both barrels. I don't go in much for stack blowing as a rule, but this last stunt of Trevelyan's was one too many. For years he'd been poor-mouthing to Grace behind Sephy's back about needing money for one desperate emergency or another. After we'd coughed up, we'd find he'd stuck Sephy and Purve with the same yarn."

The librarian harpooned another chunk of tuna. "Trevelyan was quite a con artist in his own cute way. That's how they got by, along with his moonshining and a little annuity they bought with the insurance they got from Bainbridge, their son who was lost in the war. Trev never did a tap of honest work in his life, as far as I know."

"His sons didn't get it from anybody strange then?" said Shandy. "I've heard they were both what you might call unreliable."

"I've heard them called a damned sight worse than that. If Bracebridge isn't in jail somewhere right now, he probably ought to be."

"What about Bainbridge? He must have been declared legally dead since his father collected the insurance, but is he?"

"Who knows? The way they run this ridiculous government, anything's possible. If he did survive, he's had the sense to stay away from here, anyway. Damn it, Peter, I'm so fed up with that crowd—"

Porble took a drink of water to cool himself down. "I didn't mind so much being swindled occasionally myself, but when that old shyster went after the college, I decided it was time to draw the line. So now he's apparently poisoned his wife and himself, and they're acting as if it were all my fault."

"You don't believe that yourself?" Shandy asked him.

"I'm not conceited enough to believe a few harsh words from me drove him over the edge, no. But it must have been murder and suicide. What other explanation is there? Sephy told Grace they drank whiskey laced with carbon tetrachloride. Despite my allegedly contumacious nature, I can't quarrel with the medical examiner."

"Then how do you think Trevelyan got hold of the carbon tet?"

"Who knows? Had it kicking around the house, I suppose."

"What would have been his motive?"

"To make me look bad, like as not. I told you he was loopy."

"Wouldn't he have left a suicide note saying you goaded him into it?"

"Not if he was trying to get me indicted for murder. I'm sure Minnie Mink's already told you I did them in."

Shandy didn't answer that one. "What does Persephone say?"

"I wouldn't know. We don't seem to be speaking at the moment. Well, I must get back to work. We're short-staffed since your wife's started giving her all to the Buggins Collection."

"That's what she was hired for, Phil."

"Not by me."

Porble signed his check and left without saying goodbye. Shandy finished his lunch without tasting a mouthful of it. Right here in the faculty dining room, he recalled, was where Sieglinde Svenson had got Thorkjeld to offer

Helen Marsh her job. Porble had resented the Svensons' high-handedness until he found out Helen had a doctorate in library science. After that, he'd naturally wanted to utilize her on what he deemed more important projects, notably the compilation of hog statistics. Now Svenson had plunked her back in the Buggins Room, perhaps helping to inflame Phil's smoldering anti-Buggins feeling.

Shandy didn't go much for Porble's suggestion that Trevelyan Buggins had committed murder and suicide merely to get back at his nephew-in-law for chewing him out. The man would have had to be completely around the bend for that. Nobody else had portrayed him as anything but a garrulous old coot and a fairly artful conniver. Would a wily chatterbox kill himself and his wife without at least dropping a few pregnant hints about the man he wanted to frame?

Furthermore, would Trevelyan find it necessary to die? Why couldn't he have drunk just enough of some noxious substance to make him sick, plant the seeds of suspicion and perhaps strengthen his case with regard to the lawsuit, then stay alive to enjoy Porble's downfall and collect his winnings? Maybe Trevelyan had intended to do so, but habit had got the better of him and he hadn't been able to resist pouring too generous a slug of anything that came from a bottle.

"Tommyrot," Shandy snorted aloud, to the distress of his young waiter, who thought he meant the Tuna Surprise. So he had to reassure the student that he'd only been talking to himself about something else, as absentminded professors were wont to do, and leave a bigger tip than usual to cover his confusion.

After this small contretemps, Shandy decided to soothe his nerves by strolling down to the police station and finding out what, if anything, had been learned about the Woozles. He found he'd timed his visit well. Officer Dorkin was back at the desk, sharing a hot fudge sundae with his friend Edmund.

"How did you make out at the Seven Forks?" Shandy asked him. "Great Scott, what's wrong with that cat? He's foaming at the mouth."

"Nah," said Dorkin. "That's marshmallow stuck to his whiskers. He'll lick it off sooner or later. Ed likes to save the marshmallow for last. Haul up and set. The chief'll be back in a while. He's gone to get a haircut."

"In the middle of the week?"

"Yeah, I guess he figures he might be getting his picture in the paper again. He was talking to Cronk Swope."

"Ah, then Swope's on the road to recovery?"

"I guess he's still got the cold, but his mother's going to let him out tomorrow if it doesn't storm because he's driving her nuts. She wanted to make a bunch of calls about the Friends of the Library book sale, but Cronk's got the telephone in bed with him, interviewing everybody he can think of. Hey, Edmund, quit hogging the fudge sauce."

Dorkin extracted a paw from his sundae, then resumed his report through a mouthful of ice cream. "Cronk's got his typewriter in bed with him, too, and he keeps getting the bedclothes caught in the roller. He typed half his lead article on a pillowcase Mrs. Swope's cousin Lucy embroidered for their twenty-fifth anniversary. His mother came in and saw what he was doing, and they had a big fight. Cronk wanted to get the story over to the paper, and Mrs. Swope wanted to get the pillowcase soaking in bleach before the ink got too set and wouldn't come off. She wishes to heck he'd get married and move out."

"God help the woman who gets him," said Shandy. "I gather you've completed your stint at Seven Forks. Did you detect any Woozles?"

"Oh, sure. They're all present and accounted for. Mike's the only one I didn't see. He's in the slammer, you know.

Working in the machine shop, his mother tells me. He learned a lot about mechanics holding up all those filling stations. Anyway, they don't any of them look like the Bugginses. Mike and Zack's grandmother was there, and she claims Corydon was more talk than action. She says Arbolene got sick of having to listen to all that poetry when she wanted to get down to the nitty-gritty, so she gave Corydon the mitten after a while and ran off with a tar-paper salesman from Schenectady. Want me to get hold of the FBI and see if they can put a tracer on her?"

"No, let's save the FBI for a rainy day. Good work, Budge," said Shandy, trying to hide his chagrin. Like the late Corydon, he'd been building false hopes on Arbolene Woozle.

"There is one thing, though." Dorkin didn't sound happy. "I don't know if you're going to like it much."

"I haven't liked anything so far. Don't try to spare my feelings. What's the matter?"

"Well, see, there's this Marietta Woozle who's married to Mike's brother Zack. She's a proofreader at the Pied Pica Press over in Clavaton, right next to the county court-house."

Shandy said he knew the place and what if she was?

"I'm establishing the credibility of the witness," Officer Dorkin replied stiffly. "What I mean is, Marietta has to check all the wedding invitations and Masonic installations and stuff like that to make sure they don't mix up the dates or anything, so she'd be the last person to read a number plate wrong, right?"

"Whose number didn't she read wrong?"

"Dr. Porble's."

"What?" Shandy yelped, then caught himself. "And when is she alleged not to have made this mistake?"

"At twenty minutes past nine night before last, namely February first. See, Marietta and Zack live in that red house with the white and blue trimmings, just as you turn into Second Fork. She'd been late getting home from work because the Pied Pica Press is printing the warrant for Hoddersville's annual town meeting. Marietta says there's an awful lot of proofreading in a town warrant."

"No doubt. Go on."

"So anyway, that meant she'd missed the start of the bingo. Marietta says she kind of shilly-shallied about should she go late or should she stay home and do a load of wash because she'd been looking at figures and letters all day and was pretty sick of them. But she knew her friend Ruthie would be there because Ruthie wouldn't miss the bingo if they had to carry her into the hall feet first."

Dorkin scooped out the last of the fudge sauce and gave Edmund the container to lick. "The thing was, Marietta'd flubbed up on Ruthie's birthday last Monday. She'd bought one of those cards with a turtle on it and a rhyme about being a little slow on her lunch hour, and she wanted to give it to Ruthie, so after she'd had some supper and rested her feet awhile, she pulled herself together and went."

"At twenty minutes past nine on the dot?"

"That's right. She says she looked at the clock on the dashboard as she was pulling out of the driveway, and she hadn't any more than turned when she saw this big black car with no lights on whiz out of First Fork and take a left turn toward the Junction. Marietta says she thought that was pretty strange because this was an awfully classy-looking car to be driving around First Fork in the dark. So as it slowed down for the turn, she flashed her high beams and got a good look at the number plate."

"Did she write it down?" Shandy asked unhappily.

"Oh, sure, right away. That's how she knew. She had a grocery-list pad in the car. Proofreaders have to be very methodical, she says. Anyway, she was going in late today on account of having worked overtime last night, which is how I happened to catch her home. So she gave me the number on the grocery pad and when I brought it back here, the chief called up the registry. So that's how we know it was Dr. Porble's car. I'm sorry, Professor Shandy."

Shandy was sorrier. "What did the chief say?"

"Well, first he said, 'Jeez,' then he said, 'I'll be damned,' then he said he was going to get his hair cut. I don't know why he isn't back yet."

At the word *yet*, Dorkin's voice dropped noticeably. Chief Ottermole was back. With him was Dr. Porble. Their hands were linked, but not in amity.

Chapter 12

D r. Porble was not a happy man. "Was this your idea, Peter?" he demanded nastily.

"No, it was not my idea," Shandy snapped back. "Drat it, Ottermole, are you out of your mind?"

Ottermole was the unhappiest of the lot and furious to be so. "Look, Professor, I got a duty to my job. Here's a guy who goes out an' picks a big fight with Trev Buggins. That same night, his car's seen sneakin' out o' First Fork with the lights out while the folks are upstairs an' Miss Mink's at the bingo. Next morning, both the Bugginses are found poisoned to death, an' ten minutes ago I find this in the trunk of the car, stuck down inside a box that said *Tennis Balls* on it."

Awkwardly because of the handcuff that still held him to the librarian, Ottermole reached inside his leather jacket, hauled out a longish tube, unscrewed the lid, and shook out the contents on top of the desk where Edmund was now sitting, washing the marshmallow off his whiskers. "See?"

Shandy saw. Lying beside the empty ice-cream carton was a small bottle with a dingy label that still read *Carbon Tetrachloride*.

"I s'pose you're goin' to tell me he never seen this bottle before in his life," snarled the chief.

"How the flaming perdition do I know whether he ever saw it before?" Shandy snarled back. "I may have seen the thing myself, or dozens like it. Why don't you handcuff me, too?"

"Because I got no witness that says she seen you comin' out o' First Fork night before last, because you never had a fight with Trev Buggins, an' because it wasn't your car I found the bottle in."

"But great balls of fire, man, can't you see it's a frame-up? Dr. Porble is an intelligent man. There are a good many miles of woods between here and First Fork. If he'd had his hands on that bottle, don't you think he'd have had sense enough to chuck it out the window on his way home?"

"Yeah, an' the bottle would o' made a hole in the snow an' somebody would o' seen it an' dug it out an' maybe started wonderin' who threw it there, an' why. See, Professor, that's the trouble with bein' smart. You think ahead to what might happen. Mike Woozle, now, he'd o' just heaved the bottle to hell an' gone an' never thought twice about it till he landed back in the slammer."

"Or not, as the case might and probably would be."

"Yeah, but Dr. Porble wouldn't see it that way. He didn't want anybody gettin' suspicious about what Mr. an' Mrs. Buggins died from, so he wouldn't want even the name carbon tet mentioned where it might get back to me. He was countin' on me bein' dumb enough to accept what ol' Doc Fotheringay put on them death certificates instead of orderin' an autopsy like I done. Did."

"M'yes," said Shandy. "Viewing the matter objectively, Phil, you must see that Ottermole has a certain amount of logic on his side."

"Viewing the matter subjectively," said Porble, "would you mind explaining to Grace that I'm being detained on suspicion of having murdered her relatives and shan't be home for dinner? I don't suppose she'll have time to whip up a cake with a file in it, but she might be kind enough to pack an overnight bag with my pajamas and shaving things. Assuming I'm allowed a razor, that is. What's the protocol around here, Ottermole?"

"I got an electric one you can borrow," growled the chief.

"I am overwhelmed by your consideration, though I must say I've never been able to get a decent shave with one of those contraptions."

"You have to hold it sort of head-on. I'll show you."

"Er, h'm," said Shandy. "Might we interrupt this discussion of setal severance for a moment? Phil, just for the record, would you mind telling us what you were doing at First Fork at twenty past nine on the night of February first?"

"Nothing. I've already told Ottermole I wasn't there. My wrangle with that old poop Trevelyan took place early in the morning, about half past eight. Grace had finally broken down and told me about this asinine lawsuit scheme the night before. I'd have gone straight out then and tackled Trevelyan, but I knew he'd be in bed and there'd be no point in waking him up because he'd be too drunk to talk straight. Hence the early morning row, which I freely admit to you now as I've already done before, and which Minnie Mink has doubtless told you a good deal more about than actually happened."

Porble rubbed the wrist from which Chief Ottermole had by now removed the handcuff. "I hadn't intended to lose my temper. I'd meant to discuss Trevelyan's chances of pulling off his insane plot in a dispassionate manner and try to make the damned jackass see reason, just as I tried to do with Ottermole here when he showed up at the library waving his handcuffs in my face."

"At least I didn't put 'em on till we got outside," Ottermole reminded the librarian.

"True enough, you refrained from making me a hissing and a byword in front of my staff, a circumstance for which I suppose you think I ought to be grateful.

However, I'm not sure that being made to ride in that infernal machine you erroneously refer to as a police cruiser doesn't constitute cruel and unusual punishment."

"Yeah? Then maybe you'll remember what it felt like when you get to town meeting in April an' everybody starts yammerin' about how we can't afford a new one 'cause we got to keep the budget down."

"Sorry, Ottermole. Convicted felons aren't allowed the franchise," Porble replied with a certain degree of satisfaction. "You've just lost yourself a vote."

"You're not convicted yet, Phil," Shandy reminded him. "We might avoid your felonization if we could please stick to the facts. Since you say you weren't at First Fork during the time in question, would you mind telling us where you were?"

"I was at home, naturally."

"With whom?"

"Cicero."

"Cicero who?" said Ottermole.

Dr. Porble looked pained. "Marcus Tullius Cicero."

"Jeez, why didn't you say so? How can I get hold of the guy?"

"You might try the library. I suggest you start on the Tusculan Disputations, notably Book Four, which explains how wisdom frees the mind from disquietude and thus keeps small-town cops from making stupid mistakes. What I'm endeavoring to convey, Chief Ottermole, is that I was reading a book. Alone. Solus. By myself. My wife was out. I have no alibi. You may as well put the handcuffs back on."

Ottermole could be a bastard, too. "Oh, *that* Cicero. I used to read Cicero's Cat in the funny papers myself. Budge, you slide on over to the house and ask Edna Mae for that roll-away cot we use when the in-laws come to stay. And some blankets and a clean sheet. She'll know. Tell her we got distinguished company at the lockup. Professor, when you see Mrs. Porble, why don't you remind her to put in the Cicero book?"

"Why don't we first see if we can arrive at some explanation as to how Dr. Porble's car might have been seen out at First Fork without him in it?" said Shandy. "I'm sure you realize, Phil, that Chief Ottermole's stretching things in your favor here by keeping you at the lockup instead of shipping you over to the county jail."

"I also realize that even Chief Ottermole may have some dim awareness that it's possible to be sued for false arrest," said the librarian. "Is there a bathroom, by any chance?"

"Sort of," said Ottermole. "Say, Budge, you better ask Edna Mae for a towel an' a cake o' that fancy soap she puts out when we're havin' company, too. And a can of Dutch Cleanser. Can you wait till we get the place fixed up a little, Dr. Porble?"

"No rush," said the librarian. "I'm simply trying to familiarize myself with the amenities in my new home away from home. Getting back to the subject of my car, Peter, I have no idea how it came to be seen at First Fork on the night when carbon tetrachloride assumed rightly or wrongly to have come from the bottle found in my car trunk was allegedly added to the jug from which either Trevelyan or Beatrice Buggins may or may not have poured the drinks that are supposed to have effected their joint demise. Are you with me thus far?"

"All the way."

"Good. Then I may go on to remind you that I keep my car down at Charlie Ross's Garage, as you yourself do on account of the lack of parking facilities around the Crescent, and that Charlie closes up and goes home whenever he feels like it, which is generally quite early these nights. I myself have no skill with machinery, but I'm told it's possible to perform some relatively simple operation that enables a car to be started without using the ignition key. Am I correct, Chief Ottermole?"

"Yeah," said Ottermole unhappily, "it can be done."

"Thank you. I might also mention that I leave an extra key with Charlie in case the car has to be worked on. Anybody not possessing the skill to finagle the wires might thus alternatively have broken into the station and stolen the key as a prelude to borrowing the car. As a third hypothesis, some miscreant merely took the number plate off my car and attached it to a car that looked like mine but in fact was not. No doubt our vigilant police chief can explain how any of these feats may have been accomplished and the car returned without attracting unwanted notice."

"I wasn't on duty that night," said the vigilant chief. "It was Clarence Lomax's boy Frank's turn. Frank got a call about a quarter of nine to bust up a disturbance over in front o' the Meat-o-Mat. Some kids lit a fire in the parking lot an' made believe they was going to barbecue a groundhog. Didn't amount to anything, but one o' the neighbors got all hot an' bothered an' phoned in the alarm, so Frank had to go. Can't blame a man for not being in two places at once, can you?"

"I blame nobody for anything without due and sufficient cause," Porble replied, "and only regret that the same courtesy hasn't been extended to myself. However, I'm endeavoring to respect your line of reasoning, if such it can be called, Chief Ottermole, and to accept what I trust will be my brief incarceration with what equanimity I may possess. Once released, I shall interest myself in town politics, as you suggest, and see what can be done about having you replaced by somebody who knows which end he's standing on."

Blast it, Shandy thought, this was carrying acrimony too far. Granted, Phil Porble had every right to express his dudgeon at being yanked from his august position into durance vile at a crummy lockup half the size of a chicken

coop, but couldn't he allow Ottermole a little credit for
Edna Mae's clean towel and fancy soap?

Shandy was about to tell Porble, "You're allowed to
phone Grace," but he didn't. If he went himself to break
the news that her husband had just been jugged for the
murder of her aunt and uncle, he might jolt her into
abandoning any misguided loyalty to Persephone Mink
and spilling whatever beans she was keeping under her
hat. He buttoned his mackinaw, pulled down his earflaps,
and trudged back up to the Crescent.

Chapter 13

He might have known the news would get to Grace Porble before he did. Mary Enderble was just leaving the house, wearing the sort of face people reserved for condolence calls. Even Mary, who loved everybody, didn't look happy to see him. Grace herself was downright hostile.

"Well, Peter Shandy, I hope you're satisfied."

"Great Scott, Grace, you don't think I put Ottermole up to arresting Phil?" he protested.

"If you didn't, who did?"

"Grace, Miss Mink spilled the beans about the fight with Trevelyan Buggins, to which Phil himself admits. Some woman from Second Fork has testified that she saw Phil's car with the headlights out leaving First Fork at twenty minutes past nine night before last. Ottermole himself searched the car and found an empty carbon tetrachloride bottle hidden inside the trunk. On the evidence, he had no alternative but to hold Phil for questioning."

"Peter, that's nonsense. Why didn't he arrest me instead? I drive the car a lot more than Phil does."

"I understand you were out somewhere at the time."

"I was over at the Enderbles' looking over a box of buttons John inherited from his Uncle Elijah, if that constitutes an alibi."

"What kind of buttons were they?"

"Those celluloid things you stick on your lapel, with

sayings on them like 'I Love My Wife but Oh, You Kid' and 'Remember the Maine, to Hell with Spain.'"

"And don't forget to pull the chain," Shandy murmured. "Sorry, Grace, that was crass of me. I learned that from an uncle of my own. I used to think it a scream when I was a kid."

"So did my brother Boatwright," said Grace in something like astonishment. "Goodness, I hadn't thought of Boat in ages. I wondered why it looked familiar. But anyway, Phil was right here reading the whole evening."

"So he told us. He also said you hadn't told him about the lawsuit until the previous evening. Didn't your cousin tell you before then?"

"Yes, and I was pretty upset about it myself, I don't mind telling you. I kept hoping it would all blow over, but when she said the lawyer was serving the papers or whatever they do, I knew I had to tell Phil."

"And Phil went up in smoke."

"Phil doesn't like to be put in an embarrassing position, and, I must say, neither do I. However, I knew there was no earthly use trying to talk sense to Uncle Trevelyan once he'd got a bee in his bonnet. I told Phil he'd be wasting his time, but—" Grace reached out toward the flower arrangement on the table beside her, as if for reassurance. "I'll bet it was one of the Woozles who told Ottermole that whopper about Phil. They'd love to get us in trouble."

"Why?"

"Because that's the kind they are. They've always had it in for the Bugginses."

"Grace, that would hardly be a satisfactory explanation to offer a judge."

"A judge?" For the first time, there was an edge of panic in her voice. "Peter, surely Phil won't have to stand trial for something he didn't do?"

"Not if we can come up with something more concrete than the Woozles' not liking the Bugginses."

"Well, if the truth won't serve, I don't know what will. Have you seen Phil since—?"

"Oh, yes, I just left him. He sent me up for his overnight bag."

"Peter, they're not taking him to jail!"

"No, no, nothing like that. Ottermole's holding him down at the station."

"In that awful little lockup where they put the Woozle boys on Saturday nights?"

"Edna Mae's sending over some clean towels."

"Oh, my God! What am I going to tell Lizanne?"

"Why tell her anything? Your daughter's not coming home from college this weekend, is she?"

"No, they're having a special performance of *Death and Transfiguration* at Harry Junior's school. But what if it gets into the papers?"

"How can it?" Shandy replied with well-feigned confidence. "Cronkite Swope's mother's keeping him in bed with a cold."

"But Arabella Goulson's still on the loose."

"Er, considering your personal friendship with the Goulsons and the special relationship between Lizanne and young Harry, do you think Arabella will be any more eager than you are to publicize this unfortunate development?"

Grace thought it over. "No, I don't suppose she will, though it's going to break her heart to miss a chance of scooping Cronkite. Arabella's a really dedicated newspaperwoman, you know. But she is fond of Lizanne, and you have to admit it would be a very suitable match. Not that we're anxious to get our only child married off, but to have her so well settled right here in Balaclava Junction— Peter, do you realize what this crazy stunt of Ottermole's might do to the Goulsons as well as us? Can't you get him to let Phil go? Surely there must be some way?"

"There might, if you and Persephone Mink would quit clamming up on me. Talk, Grace."

"I don't know what you want me to say."

"You might start by telling me who's actually behind this half-witted lawsuit Trevelyan Buggins is alleged to have perpetrated."

"Why do you say alleged? Uncle Trev always felt very strongly—"

"Uncle Trev felt strongly for eighty-some years, I gather, but never did anything until now. Was it his daughter's idea?"

"Of course not. Sephy wouldn't have dreamed of such a thing."

"Then who did?"

"Peter, I honestly can't tell you. Phil and I took it for granted Uncle Trev was responsible. He wasn't my uncle, of course, but I never knew what else to call him. Anyway, he was always poring over old papers of Knightsbridge's and Ichabod's. They were his father and grandfather, as I expect Helen's already told you. She knows more about the Bugginses than I do."

Grace wet her lips. "Knightsbridge never amounted to much. Neither did Uncle Trev, for all his big talk about not judging the worth of a man by his ability to accumulate worldly goods. I personally never saw anything morally uplifting about distilling rotten moonshine, which was about the only thing he ever lifted a hand to. When I was a little girl, Aunt Beatrice would be after him to fix the door or weed the garden. He'd say he would as soon as he got around to it, and she'd say, 'That'll be the day after never.' Sephy and I would wind up doing it more often than not. Or Sephy would, and I'd make believe I was helping."

"You lived with them, then?"

"For a while, after my mother died and Father didn't know what to do with me. That's when Sephy and I got to be such great friends. We'd lie in bed and talk about all the wonderful things we were going to do when we grew up."

"What about Persephone's brothers? Did you like them?"

"I can't say I ever had much chance to know them. Any more than I knew my own," Grace added somewhat bitterly. "They were all so much older, you know. That was another thing Sephy and I had in common, both of us having two bigger brothers. Of course mine weren't twins like hers, and there was a wider span between us. Boatwright must be well into his sixties now, I should think. Isn't it awful, not being able to say how old your own brother is?"

She shrugged. "But then I don't suppose Boat remembers much about me, either. He's sent me little presents once in a blue moon from different ports his ship put in at, and I used to write to him in care of the steamship line, but he never wrote back so I quit that years ago. I did send an invitation to our wedding and an announcement when Lizanne was born. He sent me a pair of carved ebony back scratchers for a wedding present with a note saying, 'You scratch his back, and he'll scratch yours.' That's about the longest letter I've ever had from him. Phil thought it was funny, but I wished Boat could have shown a little more family feeling."

Grace paused to steady her voice. "Trowbridge and his wife sent a nice gravy boat from Gump's. I did a period flower arrangement in it one year for the Boston show and won my first blue ribbon. I sent them a photo and the piece out of the paper, but all they wrote back was a postcard saying thanks for the clipping. Maybe they were offended because I used it for flowers instead of gravy. Oh, and Boat sent Lizanne one of those little Russian dolls you keep taking apart and there's another doll inside. I think that's the last I've heard from him. I've got so I just send a Christmas card myself."

"Where to?"

"I told you, the steamship line. It's the Great Magnificent, supposedly out of Liberia, but they have a New York office. I assume he's still with them. My cards don't come back."

"May I have the address?"

"I suppose so, though I can't imagine why you want it." She went over to a small rolltop desk and took out her address book, a rather sumptuous affair of green morocco with 'Grace B. Porble' stamped in gold on the cover and all the entries one hundred percent legible.

"Do you want Trowbridge's, too? We do keep in touch, more or less, though they've never come to see us or invited us out there. I'll admit Washington State's a long way from Balaclava Junction. They live in Tacoma. Trowbridge is a geologist. I believe he's always wading through swamps and climbing mountains, deciding where to build roads and things."

She handed Shandy the book, open to the B's, and sat down again with her hands on the arms of the velvet-covered chair. They were capable hands, well kept, with their nails painted a subdued apricot shade that harmonized with the chair and the rust-colored wool dress she was wearing. A modest diamond in a simple white-gold setting shot a few nicely coordinated sparks from above her matching wedding ring. While Shandy copied the brothers' addresses into the bedraggled notebook he carried around with him to keep his student appointments straight, she went on talking, more to herself than to him.

"Until I met Phil, I never really felt as if I belonged to anybody. My brothers were always away at school or camp or somewhere until they struck out on their own. I can't remember much about Mother. I was a change-of-life baby, and I don't suppose she was any too thrilled about having me in the first place. She had a stroke when I was four. Just keeled over in the kitchen one day when she was frying doughnuts. Luckily, Mrs. Horrigan—he was comptroller then and they lived where the Jackmans do now—she smelled the hot fat smoking and ran over. Otherwise, the house would probably have gone up in flames and me with it. I was upstairs in my crib, supposedly taking my nap, though I was more likely playing with my stuffed animals. It's strange that I remember my panda better than my mother, don't you think?"

"Quite natural, I should say." What other reply could Shandy make?

"So then Father took me out to board with Uncle Trev and Aunt Beatrice. I stayed there for almost two years. I don't remember Father coming to see me more than once or twice. Aunt Beatrice used to say I favored my mother, and it was painful for him being reminded. It was no picnic for me, either, but I don't suppose that ever occurred to him. People don't think small children feel things much, but they do."

She realized she was picking at the velvet and folded her hands in her lap. "Anyway, after a while, he married Judith and I came back to live with them. Judith was kind to me in her way, but she wasn't the maternal type and didn't pretend to be. She was more like a governess. But she was good for Father. They'd go out in the evening a lot and get Sephy to baby-sit me. I don't know what I'd have done without Sephy."

Damn it, what had he got himself into? Shandy wished he'd let Helen tackle Grace. But Helen must be eyeballs-deep in administrative work at the library, fretting because she was making no headway with the Buggins Collection. Great balls of fire, could Phil have been framed to keep Helen away from the archives?

Cold reason told Shandy that Dr. Porble had been framed because he'd set himself up to be eminently frameable. Getting Helen off the trail could have been seen as a possible fringe benefit, though, by somebody who knew there'd be something in the Buggins Collection that could quash the lawsuit. Considering how long the archives had been locked up at the library, that raised an interesting question.

Could Phil Porble be that subtle a conniver? Could he, despite his self-incriminating histrionics, have been the one who put old Trevelyan up to the lawsuit? Had he struck a secret deal making Grace heiress to half the profits or something like that?

Blah! If Phil had been pussyfooting through the archives and knew proofs were there, he'd have destroyed them, wouldn't he? Unless his ethics as a librarian were stronger than his honesty as a private citizen. Unless he'd meant all along for the suit to fail. Unless he planned to whip in at the last minute, drag the relevant document out of the archives, save the college from financial disaster, and make Dr. Helen Marsh Shandy look like an incompetent ninny.

What the hell for? Helen wasn't after his job. She wasn't trying to undermine his prestige. Granted, she'd exposed the boner he'd pulled in thinking the Buggins Collection a roomful of rubbish, but his predecessor had done the same. They'd both neglected the collection on the grounds that their first duty was to provide and maintain the best possible research and study facilities for students and faculty, which in fact it was and which they'd accomplished.

Besides, there was a more likely conniver right in front of him. It wasn't Phil who'd spent those early years at First Fork, who'd been steeped in Buggins family history, who loved Persephone Mink like a sister but hadn't had much use for old Trev. Grace had worked at the library, had canoodled in the stacks, had married the librarian and been privy, no doubt, to all his counsels. Lately, she'd been helping Helen some in the Buggins Room. Maybe she'd spotted something whose significance she was best suited to grasp. Maybe she was less devoted to that sarcastic bastard she lived with than their neighbors thought she was. Maybe P. Shandy had better finish off what he'd come for and get out of there.

"Is that your family?" He nodded at a photograph in an ornate silver frame that was accessorizing Grace's flower arrangement. It showed a man and woman in clothing of the late thirties, with their children. The man held a tiny girl in a fluffy white dress on his knee. Behind the parents stood two teenage boys looking resentful in jackets and ties.

"Yes," Grace answered. "I keep it there to remind myself I used to have one. People tell me I've grown to look just like my mother. Do you think so?"

"Oh, yes, no question. Your brothers favored the Bugginses, though."

"Yes, and so did Sephy's. That's another thing she and I used to giggle about, that it was our brothers and not ourselves who'd inherited the Buggins jaw."

"I saw a picture of the twins this morning out at First Fork. You said you never knew them well, but can you remember anything at all about them?"

"Not Bainbridge. He ran off and joined the army when he was still in school, or should have been. Uncle Trev had to sign some papers, I think."

"Harry Goulson told me about that. He said Bainbridge was listed as missing in action. Did his parents ever find out what happened to him?"

"If they did, nobody told me. Sephy never mentions him."

Grace fiddled with a bowl of paper-white narcissi that played the starring role in her arrangement. "No doubt Harry also told you Uncle Trev and Aunt Bea weren't exactly overcome with grief to be rid of him. Bain had been pretty wild before he went. I've always wondered how he stood the army discipline. It wouldn't surprise me if he'd simply deserted, but you needn't tell Harry Goulson I said so."

She tried a further experiment with the narcissus bowl. "I'll bet Harry gave you an earful."

"The twins seem to have left some, er, graphic memories behind them," Shandy conceded.

Grace put the narcissi back where they'd been in the first place. "Bracebridge was an awful tease. He used to tell me horrible bedtime stories about a bear coming to swallow me whole while I was asleep. He said I'd wake up in the bear's stomach and not know where I was. Naturally, I'd have nightmares and wake up in the dark and start screaming because I thought I was inside the bear. Then Brace would run in and laugh at me. Sephy used to get furious with him."

"As well she might. God, what a thing to do to a child."

"Brace could be awfully funny, though. He'd imitate the neighbors so you'd swear they were right there with you. He had a part in the senior play where he was supposed to be an older man, so he put on his makeup and costume and went all around the Seven Forks pretending to be an underwear salesman. He'd taken quite a few orders before some girl caught on to who he was. Instead of making him give back the money, she made him take her out for a rip-roaring time. Then he got drafted, and I never saw him again. He did come home for a little while after the war, but I was away at school by then."

"What's he doing now?"

"I don't know, and I'm not sure I want to. Sephy won't have anything to do with him anymore."

"Any special reason?"

"I'll say there is. As soon as Brace found out Sephy had a job and was on her own, he began writing her letters from a place in New York called the Wayfarers' Rest. He said it was sort of a shelter for people who were down on their luck, that he'd been sick and not able to hold a steady job on account of these fainting fits he was having. He wondered if Sephy could spare him ten dollars to pay a doctor. So she sent the ten dollars and naturally a couple of weeks later, he dunned her again."

Grace emitted something very like a snort. "Finally, he sent this real tearjerker. He'd fallen and broken his arm during one of his fainting fits and couldn't even dress himself. He hadn't eaten for days and was going to be turned out of his room, and if Sephy didn't wire him fifty dollars PDQ, he'd be pushing up daisies by the end of the week.

"So Sephy decided there was only one thing to do. She'd go to New York and bring him home. That was the only time in her life Sephy asked me to lend her money. I had two hundred dollars, so I gave it to her and off she went on the train, scared stiff to be traveling all that way alone when she'd never even been to Boston but determined to do her duty.

"Well, to make a long story short, she got to New York and managed to find the Wayfarers' Rest. It turned out to be a fancy nightclub. And there was her poor, sick brother, dressed to kill, out on the dance floor with some painted-up floozy, having the time of his life. Sephy gave him one look, turned around and came straight home, and gave me back my two hundred dollars. He had the nerve to write her another letter, but she threw it in the fire and then he quit.

"I shouldn't be surprised if he went right on dunning his parents, though. Every so often Uncle Trev would come to us with some hard-luck story about not being able to meet his taxes or something, which I'd know was a lie because Sephy and Purvis always kept track of the bills. We'd give him a little something if we happened to feel like it and charge it up to bread on the waters."

"Then you believe the parents had been in touch with Bracebridge all along."

"Peter, I really think you should be talking to Sephy about Brace instead of me. Right now I'm mostly concerned for my own husband. Will that lamebrain Fred Ottermole let me take Phil some supper? Or are they keeping him on bread and water?"

"You might phone the station and ask. I expect Ottermole will let you see Phil if you want to."

"Peter Shandy, you ought to be shot! Why didn't you say so in the first place? Since you're the great detective, I expect you can find your way out. I suppose I ought to thank you for coming, but frankly I wish you hadn't."

Grace was already in the next room, dialing. Shandy buttoned the coat he'd never been invited to take off and faced the gathering dusk.

Chapter 14

What was a man supposed to make of this? Had he been talking with an innocent woman in a well-merited tizzy or a Mrs. Borgia whose ill-laid plans had backfired on her own husband? Shandy had been wont to think of Grace as Porble's wife, Helen's friend, his good neighbor. There was a Burne-Jones quality about her stately good looks and her winning ways with tiger lilies that he'd admired from a respectful distance. Should he go back and ask a woman who arranged lilies if she'd happened to arrange a triple murder, too?

He'd been thinking of it as the crime of a shrewd plotter, but what if he was dealing with a series of bungles instead? Suppose that fleeting thought of his about Grace's finding something about Oozak's Pond in the Buggins Collection happened to be valid? Suppose she'd seen a way to prove the Ichabod claim legitimate or make it appear to be so? What if Grace, a fundamentally uncomplicated woman with do-gooding urges and perhaps some latent hangups from her mixed-up childhood, had decided to make her dear Sephy's early dreams come true? And what if, through her own lack of sinister cunning and Porble's unexpectedly violent reaction to the lawsuit, her plot had gone haywire?

No doubt Grace had been over at the Enderbles' looking at Chicken Inspector buttons that night, as she'd said. However, she hadn't given him a definite time when she'd left, and Shandy doubted if Mary or John would remember. Grace wouldn't have stayed late in any case. The Enderbles went to bed with the birds, and they'd have made a special point of turning in early on the first because of John Enderble's 6:00 A.M. engagement with Beauregard on the second.

Yet Porble had implied that Grace was out for the whole evening. Perhaps Porble was just being cussed, or perhaps she really had been. Grace had her own car keys. She could have picked up the car and gone out to the Forks after she left the Enderbles at, say, half past eight or even before. She could have heard about the carbon tet in Flackley's barn. Miss Mink would have brought the neighborhood trivia home from the bingo, no doubt, and the Bugginses would have repeated it because they had nothing more interesting to talk about.

She wouldn't go prowling around the place at night and risk setting the huskies off. She'd have dropped in one day to borrow a piece of dogsled harness as a container for a flower arrangement interpreting the aurora borealis or something. Any excuse would have done.

Hiding the bottle in the tennis-ball can would have made sense to Grace because only Lizanne played tennis, and Lizanne was away at school. The can had probably been kicking around the car's trunk for months. Porble wouldn't have bothered to open it. Only a simpleminded cop like Ottermole would do that. Grace wouldn't have figured on Ottermole.

She wouldn't have thought of Marietta Woozle's having to work late, either. Amateur criminals never allowed for the unexpected. Anyway, Grace wouldn't have worried much about being spotted visiting her aged relatives on the night they died. She'd come to keep them company on bingo night and found them looking poorly. No, she wasn't surprised at the doctor's verdict of death from natural causes. Only by the autopsy.

But why would she have to kill them? Because Uncle

Trev was talking too much? Because she was afraid they'd let Bracebridge get Sephy's share? Or would it be the renegade Bainbridge she had to stab? Anyway, with the rest of the family dead, everything would go to Sephy.

Could that be why Persephone Mink had refused to identify the man from the pond as her brother? If Grace had killed for Sephy, then surely Sephy could have lied for Grace.

It was an ugly theory, and Shandy didn't want to believe a word of it. He wanted to sit down with a bag of beans and count them one by one. His own house was only two doors away. Jane Austen would be glad to see him. Helen would still be up at the library, though, so it was thitherward he turned his lagging steps.

Helen was in full charge but looking frayed around the edges. She beckoned him into the librarian's office, shut the door, and bared her teeth.

"I hope you're satisfied!"

"What about?" Shandy asked, not wanting to hear.

"Sending Fred Ottermole to arrest Dr. Porble and stick me with his job."

"I did nothing of the sort," Shandy protested. "Ottermole acted on his own initiative. Look at the facts, Helen. He found the empty carbon tet bottle in Phil's car, which had been seen coming away from First Fork with its lights out on the night the Bugginses were poisoned. He knew about the fight Phil had picked with Trevelyan Buggins that same morning. With that kind of evidence, he pretty much had to put the arm on Phil. I didn't know till he'd done it. I hope to God he's mistaken, and Grace has already hauled me over the coals, so I'd thank you to lay off my wounded sensibilities."

"But what's going to happen to Dr. Porble?"

"Nothing drastic, I hope. Ottermole's being quite restrained, by his standards. When last seen, he was trying to turn the hoosegow into the Ritz Carlton with a folding cot and a bar of fancy soap."

Helen hadn't meant to laugh, but she did. "Maybe we ought to take down a flower arrangement. Is Dr. Porble allowed visitors?"

"Probably, but I'd suggest we wait till matters have simmered down a bit. Grace was on the phone with him when I left her, discussing the dinner menu. Speaking of which, what are your plans for this evening?"

"I thought I might just sit in a corner and have a good cry, assuming I ever get out of here. I'd meant to go to the visiting hours at Goulson's out of respect for Sephy, but I expect you'd rather I put in another whack at the Buggins material instead. Why does everything always have to come at once?"

"Good question," said Shandy. Through the clear glass panel in the office door, he could see the ultimate disaster impending. "Brace yourself, Helen. Here comes the president."

"Why us, O Lord?" Helen moaned. "But why isn't he roaring?"

That, thought Shandy, was another good question. Moody was not the precise word to describe Dr. Svenson's manner, but it was the best he could think of offhand.

The great man's greeting was delivered more in sorrow than in anger. "Damned shame. Sorry, Helen."

"I'm sorry too, Thorkjeld," she replied, "but I'm sure we'll soon have everything straightened out."

"Damned well better." It was more a sigh than a threat.

"You feeling all right, President?" Shandy inquired anxiously.

"No. What are you lollygagging around here for?"

"He's winning your silly old lawsuit," said Helen.

"Urrgh." But it was a spiritless urrgh. "Get Porble out first. Unseemly. Bad for morale. No reflection on you, Helen."

"And no umbrage taken. Thorkjeld, what's the matter with you?"

"It's Purvis Mink," Svenson blurted. "Came to me just now and offered to resign. Conflict of interest. Friend against friend, brother against brother. Worse than the Blue and the Gray. God damn it to hell, Purve's been on the security force ever since I got to Balaclava. Took my kids owl watching. Took *me* owl watching, blast it! Told him if he resigns, I'll resign and it'll be all his Goddamn fault if the Goddamn college goes down the tube. Got to go. Goddamn trustees' meeting."

"Shall we have a chorus of 'Just Before the Battle, Mother' before you go?" Shandy volunteered.

Svenson gave him a look. "Not funny, Shandy." But there was more spirit in his snarl and more surge in his step as he left the library.

"I think we did him good," said Helen. "Poor Thorkjeld. Running this college is an awful responsibility, Peter."

"And how adroitly he made his point that we're all in the barrel together. Do you think I'd get anywhere if I dropped over for a chat with Persephone Mink?"

"Tonight? Are you out of your mind?"

"I take it I'm to assume my query has been answered in the negative. What time might you be through here?"

"Peter, I haven't the remotest idea. Why don't you go feed Jane and make yourself a sandwich? Or stop at the faculty dining room."

"Can I bring you something?"

"With a horde of lackeys here to do my every bidding? Darling, just go."

The telephone rang. Helen gave him an absentminded kiss and picked up the receiver. Shandy went.

Jane was annoyed at having been kept waiting so long for her preprandial stroll and told him so. "Ah, you women are all alike," he replied, holding the front door for her and watching as she placed a dainty paw on the cold, wet top step, drew it back, gave it a shake and a lick, and tried again. "There's no pleasing you. Give you what you say you want, and it turns out you don't want it after all."

He was still standing there watching her pick and shake her way down the path when Jim Feldster, his next-door neighbor came along. Feldster clanked a bit, from which sound Shandy deduced he was wearing some lodge regalia or other under his overcoat.

"Hi, Pete. Walking the cat?"

"Hi, Jim. Which meeting are you off to tonight?"

"No meeting. I'm on my way to Goulson's. Trev Buggins used to belong to the August Amalgamation of Amazonians, so the brothers thought we'd give him a little send-off."

"Er, not to be rudely inquisitive, but aren't brothers the wrong sex for Amazonians?"

Feldster thought that one over for a while, then shook his head. "Oh, I get it. Always got to have your little joke, eh, Pete? You must be thinking of Amazons. I saw some in the movies once. Big, strapping girls with shin guards and bare thighs clear up to their you-know-wheres. Supposed to be warriors. Heck, who'd want to fight 'em?"

He permitted himself a mildly salacious grin before he remembered the solemnity of his mission. "You and Helen coming down later?"

"I'm not sure. Helen has to work late at the library. By the way, were you ever acquainted with either of Trevelyan's sons?"

"Nope. They were gone before we got here. I can tell you who did pal around with them, though. At least I could if I could think of his name. It'll come to me. See you later."

Professor Feldster clanked on his way. Jane Austen scurried back into the house, scolding Shandy for letting her get her paws wet. He picked her up and carried her to the kitchen.

There was roast beef in the refrigerator. Shandy had his with rye bread and pickles; Jane took hers plain. They were sharing their supper in companionable silence when the phone rang. The caller was, rather to Shandy's surprise, Jim Feldster.

"It came to me, Peter. The gink you want to see is Hesperus Hudson. He usually hangs out at the Dirty Duck out on the county road. If he's not there, they can most likely tell you where to find him."

Shandy didn't ask how his colleague, a recognized expert in fundamentals of dairy management, happened to know a gink named Hesperus Hudson who hung out at the Dirty Duck. He did say, "What makes you so sure I want to see him?"

"Why else would you have asked?" With a final muted clank, Feldster hung up. Shandy ate another pickle.

Strictly speaking, he did not want to see Hesperus Hudson. He wanted to stretch out in front of the as yet unlit living-room fire with a mild Scotch and water to wash down his sandwich, and mull things over. He decided not to light the fire, but he did allow himself a short mulling period. This somehow turned into a nap, as his mulls too often did. He awoke after half an hour or so with a stiff neck and a guilty feeling that he ought to be up and doing with a heart for any fate.

Careful not to disturb Jane, he went and got his old plaid mackinaw and his baggy tweed hat. These ought to be proper attire for the Dirty Duck. Helen still wasn't home, and he debated calling the library but didn't. It wasn't late and she had enough on her hands without an overprotective husband trying to make believe she couldn't manage without him. He scrawled her a note reading, "I've gone to whoop it up with the boys in the Malemute Saloon," and went to get his car.

Maybe Charlie Ross was an Amazonian, too. Anyway, he'd closed up even earlier than usual tonight. There was only the one dim light inside the garage to illuminate the parking lot. It would be a piece of cake to swipe a car from here, only nobody ever did because stealing cars was not the done thing in Balaclava Junction. Betsy Lomax would be sure to find out who did it because she lived right around the corner and ran the most effective bush telegraph in town.

Shandy wondered whether Mrs. Lomax might in fact know something about Dr. Porble's car that Porble himself didn't. If so, why hadn't she taken steps to make sure the car thief got his comeuppance? Betsy Lomax was no self-appointed vigilante, but she did hold firm and often expressed opinions about civic responsibility.

This time, though, there could be a conflict of interest. Mrs. Lomax must be feeling an obligation toward her friend Sephy, but she also had to consider the fact that she herself was landlady to one of Purvis Mink's fellow security guards and cousin-in-law or something to a couple more. Among the townsfolk, she was chairman of this, president of that, and related in one way or another to almost everybody. Around campus, she was the highly respected, well-paid domestic prop and mainstay to several faculty families. Shandy didn't think she'd deliberately cover up a crime involving town against gown, but she'd be a fool to open her mouth before she was damned sure of her facts.

Betsy Lomax was no fool. Sighing, Shandy started his car and headed out for the county road.

Chapter 15

Shandy was in no mood for the Dirty Duck. To be sure, he'd never been inside the place before, but he'd driven past it often enough, and past it was the obvious place to go. Scowling at its repulsive dark-brown facade, its filthy windows behind which a couple of neon signs advertising beer glowed dully in the places where they glowed at all, he could not imagine anybody going there to have a good time. They must go solely for the purpose of getting drunk.

Men—probably no women—would be slouched over the bar having endless, dreary arguments about nothing in particular. The bar itself would be chipped plastic laminate, most of its pattern worn off, smeared with dirt and puddled with stale beer. Messy ashtrays would be sitting around full of soggy, stinking cigarette butts. Maybe there'd be a bowl of stale cheese popcorn, kernels spilled over the edge by unwashed hands that had glommed into the bowl when their owners had stopped in for a couple of brews after pumping out somebody's septic tank.

It would be the kind of scene angry young dramatists liked to present to their angry older audiences as stark realism. Who the hell needed it? Not P. Shandy, for sure. He'd thought of another fish to fry. He'd get on to the next place first, giving his dinner a chance to settle, and come back later. If Hesperus Hudson was already inside here, he'd be set for the evening. If he hadn't yet arrived, why suffer the agony of having to sit there smelling the cigarette butts while waiting for him?

Shandy supposed Budge Dorkin's testimony with regard to the proofreader from the Pied Pica didn't really need to be checked, but Dorkin was young and inexperienced, and one excuse to procrastinate over the Dirty Duck was as good as another. He kept straight on to Second Fork and had no trouble, as who could, finding the white house with the red-and-blue barber-pole trimmings.

Nor was the proofreader herself far to seek. Marietta Woozle was at home relaxing. At least Shandy assumed she was relaxing. The fitted ankle-length gown she had on didn't look like the sort of garment a person would wear to check copy in. All those blue feathers around the edges of the flowing sleeves would be awfully in the way, he should think, if Mrs. Woozle tried to use her arms for anything more strenuous than peeling a grape. Shandy was reminded of the gowns Mae West used to wear in the movies he'd snuck into as a boy, except that Miss West's gowns had always shown up on the screen as black or white, whereas Mrs. Woozle's was scarlet with blue feathers. Dyed chicken feathers, he thought, but he couldn't be sure. Dan Stott would have known at a glance.

Mrs. Woozle did not go into wild jubilation at sight of a middle-aged man in a shabby mackinaw. "If you're looking for Zack," she told him drily, "he's over at the Dirty Duck."

"Er, no," said Shandy. "It's yourself I was hoping to see. You are Mrs. Marietta Woozle, I take it?"

"Take it or leave it for all I care." Mrs. Woozle shrugged, causing the blue chicken feathers to flutter in a manner that might perhaps have suggested an attempt at beguilement had the flutterer shown herself more hospitably inclined. "How do you spell Constantinople?"

Shandy supposed this might not be a particularly out-of-the-way question coming from a proofreader. Or perhaps she was doing a crossword puzzle. Anyway, he spelled it, and she nodded.

"Aha, just as I thought. You're one of those professors from the college, come to tempt me with your filthy lucre to recant my testimony about the perfidious Dr. Porble. My only reply to you, sir, is no, no, a thousand times no."

"Half that number would have sufficed," said Shandy. "I freely admit to being a professor from the college, Shandy by name, but I have no intention of trying to buy you off."

"You haven't?"

"No, no, a thousand times no. I shouldn't dream of such a thing. Anybody can see you're a woman of"—he gauged the depth of her neckline in some bemusement and settled for—"character."

"Oh."

She rested her right hand on her hip and raised the left to toy with her back hair exactly the way Mae West used to do. It was at moments like this that the older boys used to start whistling and the younger ones go out for popcorn. For an eerie moment, Shandy experienced an auditory illusion of corduroy knickers squeaking in the dark.

"What I came for, Mrs. Woozle, was simply to, er, verify a few points from the testimony obtained by Officer Dorkin earlier today. Provided you can spare the time, that is." He'd noticed her swift glance at the white hands on the blue face of the red clock on the wall.

"Make it snappy, then. What do you want to know?"

She hadn't asked him to sit down and clearly didn't intend to, although there were plenty of white vinyl chairs around, each with its starred-and-striped cushion of red and blue. She must have born on the Fourth of July, Shandy decided. He cleared his throat.

"As I understand it, Mrs. Woozle, you were on your way to the community hall at twenty minutes past nine on the night of February first. As you reached the intersection, you noticed a car with no lights on coming out of First Fork."

"Dr. Porble's car, yes."

"How did you know it was Dr. Porble's car?"

"I know the car, and I saw the number plate. I told Budge Dorkin that. Furthermore, I wrote down the number right away so I wouldn't forget it, not that I ever do. I have a photographic memory."

"Handy for you. Then perhaps you can describe the appearance of Dr. Porble's car."

She could and did. Shandy became increasingly depressed. He told himself the description didn't necessarily mean anything. Grace Porble must have driven the car over here often enough, bringing the Bugginses hot soup and flower arrangements. Marietta Woozle would have had opportunities enough to memorize its details.

But why would she want to lie about having seen it night before last? Surely she must realize the probable consequences to Porble. Mrs. Woozle didn't look to him like any half-wit, notwithstanding her blue chicken feathers. Maybe the Mae West getup was just one of those Total Woman ploys intended to lure Zack away from the Dirty Duck. As Marietta was a size or two larger than the dress, there did seem an element of overkill in her technique, but it might be that Zack was a type on whom subtleties would be wasted.

"Did you actually see Dr. Porble driving the car?" he asked in desperation.

"Well, hardly, how could I? When I flashed my high beams, I could see a shape that looked like him, sitting up tall the way he does, with sort of a Dick Tracy profile and one of those Harry Truman felt hats. I don't know anybody else who still wears one like it, so I figured that must have been him, but I'm not going to swear it was. I couldn't see the features, just a silhouette in the dark."

"I'd say you did unusually well to see as much as you did

in the flash of a headlight," Shandy told her somewhat nastily. "You must have incredible eyesight, Mrs. Woozle."

"I have," she snapped back. "In my profession, you need it. Furthermore, it wasn't just one flash of a headlight. I had my high beams on him the whole time he was pulling out and making his left turn toward the Junction, so I got both a back and a side view. Both of which are registered on my photographic mind like as if they were a videotape in the old family cassette box, and don't you think they're not. And I'll say so in front of a judge and jury if I have to. Got what you came for, Professor?"

She fluttered over to the door and held it open. Coming from a woman who stood perhaps five feet eight in her blue artificial-leather mules and must weigh in at one sixty-five or better, not counting the chicken feathers, the hint would have been a difficult one not to take. Shandy hadn't got what he'd hoped for, but he'd clearly had all she was about to give him. He mumbled, "Thanks for your time," and left. Zack Woozle's preference for the Dirty Duck, at least, had begun to make some sense.

Now that it was too late, Shandy remembered that he hadn't asked Mrs. Woozle why she was lolling around peeling grapes instead of going down to Harry Goulson's to view her former neighbors' remains along with the rest of the town. Maybe she'd felt she had nothing subdued enough to wear. Maybe she'd had another tough day over the annual warrant. Maybe she'd had enough of the Bugginses to last her while they were still alive.

Or maybe she was expecting a gentleman caller. As Shandy pulled away from the house, he noticed another car turning into Second Fork. Just for the hell of it, he pulled up on the verge once he'd got safely out on the county road, cut his engine, and got his field glasses out of the glove compartment. It was all swamp maples and alder along here, so he had a clear view through the leafless branches. Sure enough, the other car was backing up and pulling into the Woozles' turnaround.

Marietta had snapped on the outdoor light, and all he saw was Flo in her fake fur and red fright wig. Marietta didn't seem to be evincing any sign of overwhelming joy, but she was letting Flo in. As Mike's official resident lady friend, Flo might hold some kind of quasifamilial status among the Woozles. Or perhaps Marietta just welcomed any audience to unload an account of her latest real-life drama on.

They could sit over a cup of coffee in the red-and-blue dinette while Marietta gave Flo an earful about how she'd foiled the perfidious designs of the vile Professor Shandy. Flo could riposte with his comeuppance from Miss Minerva Mink. All told, Shandy wasn't cutting much of a figure around the Seven Forks. Well, he might as well turn a disastrous day into a total ruin. On to the Dirty Duck.

The roadhouse's interior was almost exactly as scabrous as Shandy had pictured it, except that he'd forgotten to include an old black-and-white television set with a totally flyspecked screen blaring away mostly unheeded on a shelf behind the bar. He ordered a beer and told the bartender not to bother about a glass. The bottle would be cleaner. Or so Shandy assumed until the bartender gallantly twisted the top off for him and wiped the neck with an unspeakable rag before shoving it across the beer-puddled, popcorn-strewn counter. There wasn't much Shandy could do except give the bottle a surreptitious wipe on his coat sleeve and send up a silent orison to whichever saint might happen to be in charge of streptococcus bacilli.

He knew better than to rush into conversation with anybody in a place like this. He took his time with the beer, which he didn't want but would have been conspicuous without, and pretended to be absorbed by whatever was happening on the television screen. Mud wrestling, from the look of it, though all Shandy could make out was the mud. As he gazed, he kept his ears open for names. He was curious to identify Zack Woozle, and he'd prefer to connect with Hesperus Hudson without having to ask who Hudson was.

Zack turned out to be no problem. He was a bit of chewed string who didn't look as if he'd stand up very well to the voluptuous Marietta, though a certain haggardness around the eyes suggested that he'd been trying to. Zack wasn't saying much, just sitting there nursing his beer and nodding automatically whenever anybody happened to throw a remark in his direction. Shandy didn't hear him speak until somebody asked him if he'd been over to see Mike lately. He said, "Nope," and went on gazing into his beer.

"Guess you been havin' a little excitement over to First Fork, eh, Zack?" somebody else remarked.

Zack nodded.

"Old man Buggins poisoned hisself and the old woman, too, I hear. Did he do it on purpose, or was it just bad booze?"

Zack shrugged.

"Bound to happen sooner or later, wasn't it? Pretty awful stuff he used to make, huh?"

"I never drunk none."

"How come?"

"Never got asked."

"Good a reason as any."

"I drunk plenty," a voice piped up from the corner.

"Huh," said Zack's interrogator. "Name me somethin' you didn't drink plenty of, long as somebody else was payin'. What you drinkin' tonight, Hesp? Cat piss an' battery acid?"

Ah, the missing link was found. Shandy listened to the inane banter another minute or two and nodded to the bartender for a second beer. While everybody else's attention was momentarily diverted to the television screen, which had somehow cleared itself in time to show a great many cars crashing into each other, he picked his way to one of the more leprous cafe tables, on which Hesperus Hudson was half reclining.

"Care for a beer, Mr. Hudson?"

"Huh?" A red eye glanced out from under the peak of a once-white painter's cap. "Who the hell are you?"

"Name's Shandy. Jim Feldster told me to look you up and say hello. You remember Jim?"

"Oh, sure."

Hesperus Hudson would have been equally ready to remember Princess Margaret or Idi Amin, Shandy thought, if they'd sent somebody over to him bearing a free beer. It was of course possible that Hudson did remember Jim Feldster because Feldster belonged to every fraternal organization in Balaclava County and a few more besides. Hesp didn't look like anybody's lodge brother, though. He looked like a dedicated barfly. He'd drained the beer before Shandy managed to find himself a chair with all its legs intact.

"Here," said Shandy, "have some of mine."

He switched bottles, figuring Hudson wouldn't be finicky about drinking after a stranger. Sure enough, Hudson wasn't.

"Thanks, pal. What'd you say your name was?"

"Longfellow," said Shandy. "Henry W."

"Yeah, that's right. I remember now. I got a phonographic memory."

"A rare gift," Shandy replied politely. "You wouldn't happen to be related to Zack Woozle's wife?"

"Zack who?"

Hesperus Hudson took a long pull at Shandy's beer. "I knew a gink named Zack once out in Frisco. He ran a Chinese laundry. Used to be a feller named Ah So that started it, but Ah went into computer stocks an' got to be a multimillionaire. So he says to hell with it, he wasn't goin' to iron no more shirts for nobody. So Zack took over. Zack Hoover, his name was. You know Zack Hoover?"

Shandy shook his head. "I'm afraid I haven't had the pleasure. But despite your, er, evident peregrinations, I understand you're a native of the Seven Forks, Mr. Hudson."

"Who you callin' a native? The Hudsons was always dyed-in-the-wool Methodists. Till I come along. I'm a freethinker. I'm a free drinker, too, when I get the chance."

Shandy took the hint and went for more beer, wondering whether he was going to get any sort of return on his bottles. The bartender gave him a thoughtful look.

"You a friend of Hesp's?"

"Nope," said Shandy. "Never laid eyes on him before tonight. Zack Hoover asked me to look him up for old times' sake, that's all. You know Zack Hoover?"

The bartender said he didn't and went to serve some loudmouth down at the other end of the bar. Shandy took the full bottles back to the unclean table and its even uncleaner occupant.

"Here you are, Mr. Hudson. I understand you more or less grew up with the Buggins twins out here."

"Who?"

"Bracebridge and Bainbridge Buggins."

"Oh, Brace an' Bain. Hell, yes. Them an' me, we was the biggest hellions ever went unhung. We used to swipe the old man's liquor. Drunk it hot out o' the still usin' a hollow reed for a straw so's he wouldn't know we was at it. Yup, first drink I ever had was right straight from Trevelyan Buggins's still. That still's a historic landmark, that still is. They ought to put up one o' them fancy signs with writin' on it."

"Who do you suppose is going to take over now that old Mr. Buggins is gone?"

"Huh?"

"Will Bracebridge come back and run the still, do you think? Have you seen him lately?"

"I see Bain now an' then."

"You do?" Shandy hoped he didn't sound too excited. "Where do you see Bain?"

"Here an' there. He comes an' goes."

"Goes where?"

"Back to get more snakes, I s'pose. Bain's always got six or eight o' them damn big pink snakes with 'im. I hate pink snakes. They remind me of Erna Millen back when we was kids. Erna Millen, fat an' willin'. Only she wasn't. I ast 'er once, an' she hauled off an' landed me one right on the kisser. Knocked out three o' my best teeth."

Shandy was beginning to suspect Hesperus Hudson had been Jim Feldster's idea of a joke. Now that he'd got stuck with the old souse, however, he might as well keep trying to get some of his beer money's worth. "What does Bainbridge Buggins do with these pink snakes?"

"Sics 'em on me. Bain was always a mean cuss. Sometimes he turns into a pink snake hisself. Dunno but what he looks more natural that way."

Hudson drained the last of his beer with a horrible slurping noise, and Shandy slid the other bottle over to him.

"Thanks, pal. Funny thing, you'd of expected it to be Brace that turned into a snake instead o' Bain. Brace was always pullin' some damn sneaky trick like that. Like as if I'm sittin' here talkin' to you an' thinkin' I'm seein' you an' all of a sudden you bust out laughin' in my face an' you're Brace all the time. You sure you ain't Brace? Seems to me I did see Brace lately. He was passin' hisself off as Henry Wadsworth Longfellow."

"Henry Wadsworth Longfellow? What in Sam Hill makes you say that?"

"I seen Henry Wadsworth Longfellow. I mean, I seen pitchers of 'im. See, over in Middlesex County they got a place they call the Wayside Inn, which it ain't. It's the Red Horse Inn, an' before that it was somethin' else. But anyways, it's where this here Longfellow was s'posed to have done 'is heavy drinkin' an' wrote 'is pomes, so they got this room they call the Longfellow Room an' they got pitchers of 'im all around. Got a taproom, too. I had me one o' them old-time drinks they call a coow woow. Whoo! So I had me a few more. That was when I was young an' reckless."

"So in short, you recognized your old friend Bracebridge Buggins from portraits you'd seen of Henry Wadsworth Longfellow at the Wayside Inn in Sudbury," said Shandy. "That makes sense, I suppose. What were the, er, distinguishing features?"

"Huh? Oh. Well, see, Brace had this big bushy white beard clear down to 'is belt buckle, an' he was wearin' this funny-lookin' old black suit with long coattails to it."

"Did you ask him why?"

"Nope, no sense in askin'."

"Why not?"

"He was dead."

Shandy tried to keep his voice level. "Are you sure of that? He didn't, er, turn into anything and disappear?"

"Nope. He just laid there."

"There where?"

"Same place we always used to go. That shack in the woods where Brace's ol' man run his still."

Great balls of fire, could Hudson possibly be telling the truth? "Did you touch him, Mr. Hudson? Try to take his pulse or anything?"

"I didn't take nothin'. Nothin' to take. I tried the still first, see, thinkin' there might be a swig or two left in the bottom, but she was dry as an old maid's tit. So then I figured I better see if there was anything in Brace's pockets. Like maybe a bottle or the price of a drink."

"And was there?"

"Nope. Not a damn blasted thing 'cept a couple o' rocks."

Chapter 16

"Great Scott!" cried Shandy. "Are you positive it was Bracebridge?"

"If it wasn't him, then who the hell was it?"

"Not Bainbridge, by any remote chance?"

"He didn't have no pink snakes with 'im."

The old soak leaned even farther across the table and blew a gust of ill-digested alcohol in Shandy's direction. "Look, mister, I know when I'm seein' things an' when I ain't. If that'd o' been Bain, I wouldn't o' bothered tryin' to fish through his pockets, would I? 'Cause anybody that can turn into a snake ain't got none, see."

"M'well, you may have something there, Mr. Hudson. All right, then, you did in reasonably sober fact see a human being in the still house whom you were satisfied was Bracebridge Buggins. You felt his body."

"I never. All I done was go through that ol' black suit he was wearin', like I said. There wasn't nothin' in the pants pockets, only the coat. I couldn't find them at first. Turned out they was in the coattails, where you'd least expect 'em."

"Was he lying on his back or on his face?"

"On 'is back. That's why I thought at first he was Henry Wadsworth Longfellow, see. I seen that big beard an' the funny clothes an' I says to myself, that's the feller I seen at the Wayside Inn. An' then I says, no, by God, it's Brace Buggins dressed up an' tryin' to make a fool out o' me."

"You didn't make any attempt to rouse him?"

"Hell, no, what'd I want to do that for? I told you I was

tryin' to pick 'is pockets. Anyways, I knew he was dead. His mouth was open an' his eyes was starin' an' he was stiff as a new boot. See, one arm was like this."

Hudson crooked his own left arm and raised it shoulder high. "An' when I went to raise 'im up a little so's I could get at the back pockets, which turned out to be a waste o' time like I told you, that arm didn't even flop. He come all of a piece, as you might say."

"Then, in fact, you did handle the body," said Shandy.

"Well, I didn't go pawin' it all over like Erna Millen used to do. Or so Brace claimed, but o' course Brace would say anything."

"I understand. So then what did you do?"

"Hightailed it the hell out o' there an' went back to my own place. I had a bottle o' lemon extract stashed away that I'd lifted from the general store in case of emergency."

"Extremely foresighted of you, Mr. Hudson. Where do you live?"

"I got a shack out in the woods 'bout halfway between Buggins's an' here."

"Ah, yes, strategically located between the sources of supply. Would you care to take a little ride with me?"

"Where to? Hey, you ain't one o' them do-gooders wantin' to take me someplace an' dry me out?"

"I shouldn't dream of taking such a liberty. It's just that I know where we can get better liquor than we're drinking here."

"Won't cost me nothin'?"

"Not a cent."

"Good, 'cause that's just about how much I got to spend."

Hudson was still reasonably steady in his pins, Shandy was relieved to see. Getting him over to the door was no problem, but it would have been foolish to hope their departure could be effected without some comment from the drinkers at the bar.

"Hey, Hesp, where you goin'?" the bartender wanted to know. "Steppin' out in high society all of a sudden?"

"We're just going to pay a little call on an old friend," Shandy answered for Hudson. "Don't worry, sir, I'm not aiming to deprive you of a steady customer."

"You tryin' to be funny?"

The inquiry came from a big fellow sitting rather closer to the door than Shandy wished he were. Without seeming to be in any great rush, Shandy managed to steer Hudson outside before a fracas got rolling. He even had time to notice that Zack Woozle was still among those present, still scrying for who knew what in the depths of his still unfinished beer.

"My car's over here, Mr. Hudson," Shandy said.

His guest stared at the vehicle and reared back like a stricken coyote. "Jesus, mister," he muttered, "where'd you steal this one?"

"It's mine, all bought and paid for," Shandy reassured him. "I, er, struck a lucky patch awhile back."

Not luck but years of careful work had brought forth the world's most magnificent rutabaga, the Balaclava Buster, from which the Shandy fortunes were in large part derived, but he saw no reason why he had to file a financial report with Hesperus Hudson. His one aim was to get the man over to Harry Goulson's and see whether Hudson could make a firm identification of the body in the refrigerator.

And after that, what? The humanitarian thing would be to tuck the drunk up for a comfortable night in the lockup, give him a decent breakfast, then deliver him back to his customary haunts with a few dollars' drinking money in his pocket. Shandy couldn't see Phil Porble taking kindly to Hudson as a bedfellow, though. In any case, the lockup was hardly big enough for the two of them, and Edna Mae Ottermole might not have another roll-away cot to spare.

Well, he'd manage one way or another. Right now,

Hudson appeared to have reacted to the unaccustomed luxury of the car's upholstery by falling asleep, which was all to the good. Shandy himself would have done the same, if he hadn't had to drive.

He felt as if the evening should be far spent, but it turned out not to be. When they got to Goulson's, he saw visitors still coming and going, though mostly going. The master of the obsequies was less than overjoyed to see Professor Shandy wandering in with a stinking stumble-bum in tow, demanding to view the unknown remains in the fridge.

"Why don't you folks go make yourselves comfortable in the back parlor till I can get to you?" Harry Goulson suggested in a gallant effort at cordiality. "I'm pretty sure there's still some coffee and doughnuts left."

"Coffee an' doughnuts?" yowled Hesperus Hudson. "You told me we was goin' to get free booze."

"We'll get it," Shandy tried to reassure him. "I just want you to take another look at that body while you can still see straight."

"What the hell for? I already seen it straighter than I wanted to. An' I didn't like the looks of it then, an' I won't like it any better now."

"But you'll get your name in the papers. Think of the glory."

"Huh. I already had my name in the papers plenty o' times. Mostly for bein' drunk an' disorderly. Used to be for drivin' under the influence, but I ain't druv since nineteen fifty-two. Got my license took away so many times I figured the hell with it an' quit. Damn cars they build nowadays ain't worth stealin', anyways. You ain't foolin' me none with that fancy tin can o' yours, mister, an' you needn't think you are. Free whiskey, huh!"

Hudson slumped into a chair and took a swig of the coffee Shandy handed him. "At least it's wet," he admitted in a somewhat less belligerent tone.

"Have some more," Shandy urged. "And a doughnut. Lots of doughnuts." He had no illusion that a few cups of coffee would make any dent in the kind of bun Hesperus Hudson had spent all these years laying on, but at least they wouldn't make the old soak any drunker.

Silvester Lomax, co-chief of the college security guards, was filling in for Purvis Mink tonight but had taken time to stop down on his coffee break and pay his respects. When Lomax stepped out to the back parlor for a cup of coffee just so nobody could accuse him of taking his break under false pretenses, Shandy asked if he'd mind keeping an eye on a material witness for a few minutes. Lomax said he didn't, so Shandy left him with Hudson and went out front.

A few stragglers were still around, condoling with the Minks and admiring the Goulsons' handiwork. Persephone looked about ready to be laid out herself by now. In fact, Shandy thought the elder Bugginses looked better than she did. Better than they'd looked in years, like as not. Goulson had rushed in a double casket from Boston, so in death they were not divided. Arabella had tucked a single white rose into the waxen hands folded across the old lady's violet polyester bosom. Trevelyan Buggins was holding what had presumably been his favorite pipe, polished and deodorized as he had surely not kept it during his lifetime. Why not a vinegar jug, Shandy thought pettishly.

Both loved ones were wearing their trifocals. The eyeglasses were presumably supposed to make them look more natural, notwithstanding the fact that they were lying down with their eyes shut. Every new undertakers' wrinkle seemed to take the deceased another step back toward ancient burial customs. Shandy wondered if they each had a Susan B. Anthony silver dollar tucked under their tongues to pay for the ferry ride across the River Jordan, but he thought he wouldn't ask.

He'd hoped to get a word in with Persephone Mink, but there didn't appear to be much hope of that just now. Having him loose in the main parlor evidently worried Harry Goulson, though. Goulson made a quick decision to leave the official hovering to his wife Arabella, who often hovered for him when the boy wasn't around to help out, and get the potentially troublesome Shandy out of there before the back-room dilemma developed into a front-room catastrophe.

"I can spare you a few minutes now, Professor," he murmured. "This way, please."

By now, Hesperus Hudson was having a pleasant chat with Silvester Lomax and didn't much want to break up the party, but Lomax said he had to get back to work, anyway. They parted amicably, and Shandy at last got to show Hesperus Hudson the body in the drawer. Hudson at once protested.

"That ain't Henry Wadsworth Longfellow. Where's his whiskers?"

"Right here." Goulson produced the whole armload, nicely dried and fluffed, and fitted it on the clean-shaven face.

"Is that how you saw him?" Shandy asked.

"Yup," said Hudson, "only he was layin' on the floor o' the shack with his coattails spraddled out beside 'im. An' he didn't look so neat."

"I've tidied him up some," Harry Goulson admitted. "I couldn't help it, Professor. My professional ethics were involved."

"Quite understandable," said Shandy. "So it was a false beard. Must have been stuck on pretty tight to have resisted coming off in the water."

"It was," said Goulson. "I had a heck of a time with it. I better not tell you how I got it off."

"No, don't," said Shandy. "What about the hair?"

"Oh, that's his own. No question."

"Brace always did have a fine head o' hair," said Hudson. "Never thought he'd be the type to grow a beard, though."

"But wouldn't it be consistent with his liking to dress up and fool people?" said Shandy. "And it isn't a real beard, you know."

"It isn't?" Hudson picked the mass of white hair off the dead man's face and chest and held it up for a closer look. "Seems real enough to me. What you mean is, it's real but it ain't his. Jesus, wouldn't that be just like Brace? Swipe a man's beard an' then laugh in his face from under it. Boy, he sure was a cough drop."

"Then you're still convinced this is Bracebridge Buggins's body?" Shandy pressed.

"How the hell do I know? Brace might o' stole that, too."

"Er, assuming he didn't, can you say it resembles Bracebridge Buggins as you knew him?"

"What kind o' dumb question is that? When I knew Brace, he was a young kid growin' up. This here's an old man, or close to it. All I'm sayin' is, it looks like I figure Brace ought to look if he was as old as he is now."

"I stand corrected," Shandy replied meekly. He must be even more tired than he'd thought he was. "Would there be any, er, distinguishing mark by which we could make a positive identification? A birthmark, for instance, or an old scar he acquired as a boy?"

Hudson was trying on the beard and had to untangle his mouth from quite a lot of straggly false hair before he could answer. "Cripes, that's awful-tastin' stuff. Sure, Brace had a scar, right under the jawbone. I gave it to 'im myself one day when I was tryin' out my first pair o' brass knuckles. They was Bain's to start with, but he sold 'em to me for a buck an' a half 'cause he'd took another pair he liked better off'n a guy he got into a fight with at the county fair."

"I didn't notice any scar when I took the whiskers off," said Goulson.

"Perhaps it was a less, er, permanent memorial than Hudson thought," said Shandy. "Scars do fade with age oftentimes. Have you a strong light we can shine directly on the face, Goulson? And a magnifying glass, by any chance?"

Goulson had both, the magnifier being the kind one slips over one's head like a pair of welder's goggles. It came in handy sometimes, he explained with considerate vagueness.

But it availed Shandy not at all. "I can't see any sign of a scar."

"Maybe he got it took off," Hudson suggested. "They do them kind of operations now by plastered surgery. They was talkin' about it one night over at the Dirty Duck."

"Even the most expert plastic surgeon may leave scars visible to the trained eye," said Goulson. "May I, Professor?"

"Feel free." Shandy turned the goggles back to their owner, but Goulson's professional expertise failed to turn up any evidence that there had ever been a scar on the spot Hudson indicated.

"Then this must be Bain after all," said Hesperus Hudson. "Only what the flamin' heck did he do with all them pink snakes?"

"It's still arguable that the scar, er, wore off," Shandy insisted. "You see how deeply lined and creased his skin is. That would be from exposure to wind and sun, wouldn't you say, Goulson?"

"Yeah, but Brace always used to wear one o' them long white silk scarves," Hudson argued. "Like them flyin' aces in the old movies."

"I thought you'd decided this must be Bainbridge." Peter Shandy was exasperated and showing it. "By the way, what color were the twins' eyes?"

"Why don't you open 'em an' find out?"

The coffee and doughnuts must be having a somewhat too stimulating effect on however much might be left of Hesperus Hudson's brain. Hesp must have had to have been a real wise guy back when he and the twins were helling around together.

"This is a test question," Shandy told him severely. "I'm asking you what color the Buggins boys' eyes were. Can you remember?"

"I can't even remember what color my own eyes were," snarled Hudson. "When do I get that drink?"

Shandy decided he might as well throw in the sponge. "Would you happen to have anything alcoholic in the house, Goulson? It doesn't matter what. Sorry to have put you to all this trouble."

"That's quite all right, Professor. I'm more anxious than you are to have that man identified."

Goulson fished in a cupboard and brought out a fifth of Seagram's and a clean glass, into which he poured a generous slug. "Here you go, Mr. Hudson. I always keep some on hand out here. In my profession, we never know when somebody's going to need a corpse reviver in a hurry. Want a little water with it?"

Hesperus Hudson glared at the undertaker as if he'd been a large pink snake. "If you mentioned that word at the Dirty Duck, they'd throw you out for unbecomin' conduct."

He drained the glass and held it out for more. Harry Goulson glanced at Professor Shandy, shrugged, and poured a refill. Then he capped the bottle and set it back in the cupboard.

"Cheapskate," grunted Hudson. "Looks like I better make this one last." He pulled up a chair to the embalming table, spilled a few drops of his drink, just enough to make the place look homey, and slumped over the puddle in what must have been his customary attitude.

Shandy and Goulson left him there and went back to the main parlor. By now, the visitors were all departed. Arabella was helping the Minks, their daughters, and an assortment of in-laws into their coats. This probably wasn't the right time to bother Persephone, but Shandy did it anyway.

"Mrs. Mink, we've got a chap out back who seems pretty well convinced that dead man we haven't been able to identify yet is one of your brothers. He claims to have known them both well when they were youngsters together. His name is Hesperus Hudson. Are you acquainted with him yourself?

"Why, yes, of course. The Hudsons lived over at Fourth Fork. None of them ever amounted to much, as far as I know," she added with a sniff. "Last I heard of Hesp, he'd turned into a real down-and-outer. They say all he does now is hang around the Dirty Duck trying to find some sucker fool enough to buy him a drink."

"But he did pal around with your brothers?"

"Which was no compliment to them. Or to him, either, I have to admit."

"So what it boils down to is that Hesperus Hudson might have known Bracebridge and Bainbridge even better than you yourself did, considering the difference in your ages."

Persephone gave Shandy a grim nod. "A good deal better, I shouldn't be surprised. Not that goodness had anything to do with it, as Mae West used to say. Nice way for me to be talking here." She glanced around at the two elder Bugginses in their flower-banked casket. "I always had a hunch it was the three of them who broke into the soap works that time and set off the sprinklers."

"That would have had to be just before Bainbridge went into the army, wouldn't it?"

"I shouldn't be surprised if that was why he went. An awful lot of damage was done. The factory owners were all set to prosecute right up to the hilt if they'd ever been able to catch the ones who did it. Bain most likely got scared and ran away before Brace could turn him in for the reward. He was an awful coward, as most bullies are."

She sniffed again. "I remember how glad I was to see him go. I was only a little girl at the time, but I could tell Mama and Daddy were just as pleased as I was, though they put a better face on it. Mama was singing 'God Bless America' the day she hung that flag with the gold star on it in the window to show the neighbors her son had given his life in the service of his country. She'd bought it the day he was shipped out, just in case. That was about the only thing Bain ever did that gave her any real satisfaction, that and the insurance money. Hesp isn't trying to make you believe that's Bain back there, is he?"

"He seemed fairly well convinced it's Bracebridge, except that he claims Bracebridge had a scar on his jawbone that we can't see any trace of. Do you recall such a scar?"

"No, I don't. All I can say is, if Brace ever did have such a scar, he'd have gone to considerable pains to hide it unless he changed a lot over the years. He used to be awfully vain of his looks, as I remember him. He claimed he was the handsome one of the twins, though I myself never noticed much to choose between them. It was mostly that Brace was always fussing over his hair and his clothes, while it was all Mama could do to make Bain take a bath and change his underwear once in a blue moon. I expect the army straightened Bain out on that nonsense, though."

"Not for long," her husband grunted.

Purvis Mink was typical of the Balaclava security guards, Shandy thought. He was medium-sized, spruce without being dapper, and somewhat weather-beaten, like the man in the back room, since he spent so many of his working hours out of doors. Mink would have scorned to be called handsome, but he wasn't a bad-looking man for his age, which must be in the upper fifties by now.

"I take it you never knew the twins, Mink?" Shandy asked him.

"Nope, never laid eyes on either one of 'em to the best of my knowledge," the guard replied, "and can't say I ever missed 'em. I only met Sephy when she and Grace moved into the cottage up above the campus. Sorry I can't help you out, Professor, but it's nice of you to take an interest. Now if you don't mind, I think we ought to be moving along. Sephy's pretty well tuckered out. Seems to me I had a hat when I came in, Arabella."

"A gray one," said Persephone.

"Mrs. Goulson fished around in the coat closet. "Oh, dear, Purvis, I'm afraid the only hat left here is brown."

"That's it," said Mink.

His wife blushed. "There I go again. I'm sorry, Arabella."

"Think nothing of it, Sephy, dear," her fellow garden clubber replied with a smile. "It's not like that time at Commonwealth Pier after the flower show when you had us all traipsing back and forth around that huge parking lot looking for a gray car and it turned out to be brown. My Aunt Luanna had the same problem. Brown looks gray to you because you can't see the red in it. And not being able to see red is what makes you so sweet-tempered."

Shandy hated to spoil Arabella's bit of fun, but it did raise an interesting question. "Er, if you'll forgive me for mentioning it, Mrs. Mink, how could you be so sure about your brother's eyes yesterday morning?"

"I said they were brown, didn't I?"

"Yes, but you can't see brown."

"I can see blue all right. That man's were blue, weren't they?"

"Yes," Shandy had to admit.

"Then that lets Brace out, as I told you in the first place. His were brown. He said so himself, once when I asked him."

Chapter 17

"We won't worry about that one till we get this pair here buried," said Purvis Mink with gruff tenderness. "Come on home, Sephy."

"It's bedtime for me, too." Arabella Goulson clearly felt she'd hovered long enough. "You won't be long, will you, Harry?"

She was too well mannered to give Professor Shandy a look, but he was left with the distinct impression that a look had been given. Her husband cleared his throat.

"What are you planning to do with Hesp Hudson, Professor?"

"Frankly, I've been wondering about that myself," Shandy admitted. "There's no room in the lockup, unless Ottermole's had a change of heart about Phil Porble."

"Which he hasn't," Goulson half groaned. "Grace was in to pay her respects a while back, and she looked pretty glum, I can tell you. But you know Grace—she'd hold her head up no matter what. The wife and I are pretty worried about Phil ourselves, I don't mind telling you. Aside from everything else, there's Lizanne and the boy to think of. I asked Grace on the QT if she'd told Lizanne yet, and she said no, she hadn't had the heart to spoil the kids' big weekend. Well, I expect it'll all get straightened out in a day or so. Won't it?"

What the hell was Goulson asking him for? Shandy supposed even an undertaker needed a little consolation

165

now and then. "I hope so, Goulson," he said. For whatever that was worth.

"You don't suppose, Professor, there's any chance Trevelyan Buggins and his wife what you might call effected the departure of their loved one themselves? Not that they mightn't figure they had good and sufficient reason, from all I've heard of the Buggins boys, but they might nevertheless have been overtaken by remorse afterward, him being their own son, after all, and, well—"

"Effected their own departures, too?"

Shandy didn't try to suppress his next yawn. It wasn't the kind that can safely be bottled up. "Having first arranged with Phil Porble, you mean, to dump the son's body in Oozak's Pond on the night of February first so it would be there to provide a spot of extra excitement at the Groundhog Day doings? M'yes, that would tie everything up nicely, wouldn't it? Do you suppose Persephone Mink would feel any better if we called her up and asked her what she thinks of the idea?"

"It was only a passing notion," Harry Goulson replied somewhat huffily. "I don't suppose you realize it, Professor, but there's something pretty darned upsetting to a man in my profession, having an unknown loved one cluttering up his refrigerator."

"No, I hadn't quite realized it," Shandy admitted, "but I can see that it might be."

Thus encouraged, Goulson warmed to his topic. "And when you've been given reason to believe he might be a known after all but nobody seems to be sure which known, that only makes it worse. We Goulsons have always prided ourselves on friendly service to our friends and neighbors, but it's awfully hard to work up much friendly feeling toward somebody that you don't know who he is. 'Specially when he's been murdered. I don't mean to complain, Professor, but I can't help having a feeling that this particular stiff has overstayed his welcome. Which brings us back to the subject of Hesperus Hudson."

"All right, you've made your point, Goulson. I'd drive him home if I knew where he lives, but from what he told me, it's just a shack in the underbrush somewhere between Buggins's still and the Dirty Duck. I can't say I'm keen on gong out to look for it at this time of night. I can't put him in the lockup because Phil Porble's in residence there. I can't take him home because my wife's got our guest room, such as it is, crammed full of the Buggins Archive, and I'm afraid she'd take umbrage in a big way if I parked him on the living-room sofa. Normally, we put up unexpected guests at the College Arms, but I don't know how Mrs. Blore would react to Hudson."

The College Arms was the somewhat pretentious name of an ultrarespectable boardinghouse run by a third cousin of Betsy Lomax and catering mostly to stray professors and visiting parents. In fact, Shandy knew exactly how Mrs. Blore would react to Hesperus Hudson, and so did Goulson. The undertaker sighed.

"I wish I could help you out, Professor, but I'm pretty tied up here, what with the double funeral tomorrow morning. Best thing I can suggest is that you take Hesp over to Zack Woozle's. Marietta's his niece. I expect she'd know what to do with him."

"Thanks, Goulson." Shandy tried to keep the bitterness out of his voice. "Now if I can just get him out to the car—"

"I've got that rolling table I use to cart the loved ones around on."

This proved not to be needed. Hesperus Hudson was still able to roll a bleary eye and push his glass hopefully across the table. Shandy shook his head.

"No more tonight, Mr. Hudson. I'll give you some drinking money for tomorrow, but right now I'm going to take you home."

"Dirty Duck," Hudson insisted.

That would have been fine with Shandy. The trouble was, by the time they'd got back out there, the cars were gone and the door was locked.

"Closed for the night," Shandy groaned. "Where's your shack, Hudson?"

"Huh?"

"Your shack. The place you live in. Where is it?"

"In there." Hudson waved his arm in a gesture that included most of the Seven Forks.

Shandy stared gloomily out the car window at the expanse of slush and brush in which he had no intention of getting stuck. "Come on, I'll drop you at your niece's."

"Leave me here."

"You'd be frozen to death by morning." And not a bad idea, either, but Shandy didn't want to be the one responsible. It would have to be the Woozles', though the thought of Hesperus Hudson amid all that shining vinyl was mind-boggling.

It was clear even before Shandy got Hudson pried out of the passenger seat that they couldn't have arrived at a less opportune time. Despite what looked to be an efficient job of weatherproofing around the doors and windows, he could hear the hitherto silent Zack bellowing like an infuriated gnu.

"You needn't think I don't know what you've been up to."

"Yeah?" Marietta was giving it back to him, hot and heavy. "Listen, Buster, if you were up to it yourself once in a while, you wouldn't have to be so Goddamn worried about whether I was getting it from somebody else."

Shandy had to listen to a number of improvisations on the same theme before he'd managed to drag Hudson up to the door and make his pounding and hammering heard over the bedlam inside.

"Who the hell is it?" Zack roared at last.

"Why don't you go find out, you lazy bum?" screamed Marietta.

"Why don't you go yourself, you sleazy slut?"

"Oh, Christ on a crutch!" Shandy joined his own voice to the pandemonium. "Open up in there. It's the police."

That got him some action. Zack Woozle hurled the door open. "What the hell do you want?"

"I want you to take your drinking buddy off my hands so I can go home and go to bed."

Shandy spun the by now comatose Hesperus Hudson across the waxed red-white-and-blue linoleum like a skep on a curling rink and ran for his car before the Woozles could get their wits together and scoot the old sot back.

Not that it was any of his business, but he couldn't help wondering whom Marietta Woozle had been entertaining. With all her screaming just now, he'd noticed that she hadn't once come straight out and denied her husband's accusations. Her proofreader's code of ethics must balk her of any flagrant inaccuracy. It would have had to be somebody local, anyway. No Don Juan in his right mind would travel far on a night like this just to get tickled by a lot of blue chicken feathers.

"*Seductio ad absurdum,*" he murmured and switched on the car radio to keep himself awake.

It was with ineffable relief that he at last unlocked the door of the little brick house on the Crescent. He'd expected Helen would be asleep, but she called down the stairs, "Peter, is that you?"

"Nay, my love," he replied. " 'Tis but a pallid wraith of the dashing fellow you once knew. I thought you'd be well away to the Land of Nod by now."

"So did I, but it's been a busy evening. Grace Porble just left a short while ago. She's in a state, Peter."

"Who isn't? Want a cup of cocoa?"

"No, thanks. I must have drunk six cups of tea with Grace. I didn't dare offer anything alcoholic for fear she'd fall apart completely."

"And how right you were to refrain. Getting yourself

stuck with a helpless drunk is one hell of a fix to be in. I speak from recent personal experience."

"So that's what you've been up to." Helen was downstairs now, in a padded apricot silk robe Shandy had given her for Christmas, with her head buried against his old gray cardigan. "Phew, you smell like a barroom."

"Like the Dirty Duck, to be precise."

"Not that awful dive out on the old county road?"

"How do you know it's an awful dive?"

"Anybody can tell just by looking at the outside. What were you doing there, for goodness' sake?"

"Goodness, as your friend Sephy Mink remarked a while ago in Harry Goulson's front parlor, had nothing to do with it."

"Peter, she didn't! Sephy would never in the world say such a thing at her own parents' funeral."

"It was not at the funeral. It was at the lying-in-state, or whatever they call it these days, after the visitors had gone and she was free to let down her hair a bit. Nor were the words uttered in a spirit of levity, as you appear to have erroneously surmised."

"Peter, darling," said Helen, "our marriage until now has been, on the whole, a remarkably happy one. Would you care to keep it that way, or do you want me to begin shrieking like a shrew?"

"I'll opt for continued harmony, since you're kind enough to offer the choice. I've had one run-in with a shrew already."

"My, my, you have been making a night of it, haven't you? Shall we hold an experience-sharing session?"

"How about if we just hold each other? All this prowling around late at night is setting Jane a bad example."

"Don't try to humbug me. Cats are nocturnal animals, like husbands on the loose. What have you been up to?"

So Shandy told her, scattering garments around the bedroom as he talked. "And now I'm going to take a shower and chew a couple of cloves and hit the sack. 'For the sword outwears the sheath and the soul outwears the breast, and the coat outwears the pants till there's nothing left but the vest.' First half Byron, second half some greater poet whose name I can't recall offhand. Not Corydon Buggins, that's for sure. Come on, Jane, you can climb the shower curtain while the old man ablutes."

"Take his dirty socks and underwear with you, Jane, and stuff them in the laundry hamper," Helen suggested through a yawn. "And bury those awful old trousers in the kitty box."

"Shrew!" Shandy removed the offending garments and went to wash off the clinging effluvia of the Dirty Duck. Then, snug in clean pajamas and warmed by a sweet conjugal form, he lay trying to sort out the scramble in his mind.

Was it one of the twins down there taking up room in Goulson's icebox or just a stray body Bracebridge had stolen along with the beard, as Hesperus Hudson had suggested? Had Captain Flackley shown up at the funeral parlor tonight, or had he been otherwise occupied? And did the occupation, interesting thought, have anything to do with Marietta Woozle? Maybe it wasn't Mae West she'd been trying to impersonate but a patriotic penguin. Thinking of penguins, Shandy fell asleep.

He'd probably have slept until noon if Helen hadn't set the alarm clock for seven. "Sadist," he groaned. "Is there no compassion in your bowels?"

"People aren't supposed to use words like bowels in polite conversation. My mother says it's rude," she replied. "One of us has to work today, in case you'd forgotten. Me first in the shower."

"Go ahead. I'm clean enough already."

He was all set to settle back for a little more sack time, but Helen had other plans for him. "Then you can cook breakfast. Bacon and two eggs for me, please. Goodness knows when I'll get any lunch. You were planning to get poor Dr. Porble unjugged today, were you not? I don't see how I can handle his job and my other responsibilities much longer."

"Am I then to construe his continued incarceration as a threat to my connubial privileges?"

"I hadn't quite thought of it that way, but what a splendid suggestion."

Helen shut herself in the bathroom. Cursing the unsportsmanlike behavior of Dame Fortune, Shandy went down to the kitchen.

He had two classes to teach this afternoon. Tomorrow was booked solid with morning and afternoon laboratory sessions in the experimental greenhouses. That gave him a bit less than six more hours to get Phil Porble sprung and somebody else arrested for three murders.

At least Hesperus Hudson's testimony had pretty well clinched the connection between the first man's death and the other two. Pink snakes Hesp might see, but rocks in the pockets of an old-fashioned tailcoat worn by a man got up to look like Henry Wadsworth Longfellow were not the sort of hallucination likely to be visited upon even a steady customer of the Dirty Duck. Not when he'd seen it on premises belonging to a man well versed in the works of Corydon Buggins and not when a corpse perfectly answering Hesp's description had been fished out of Oozak's Pond in front of about half the inhabitants of Balaclava Junction and its environs.

Hudson had demonstrated that at least part of his mind was still in working order, perhaps because he never had money enough to stay as drunk as he preferred to be. His story of why he'd gone to the shack and how he'd found the body rang true enough. Too bad he couldn't recall exactly when he'd gone there, but Shandy had got the impression it was within the past week or two. That would be about the right span of time for the body to have been in the pond. Much longer, and the false beard would surely have come loose regardless of what it was fastened with, because the facial tissues would have begun to deteriorate.

The still had been bone dry, Hudson had said. Shandy believed that, too. Having virtually grown up on Buggins's moonshine, Hudson must know how to go about extracting any possible deposit of dregs from its workings. That meant it had been some time since old Buggins had run a batch through. Alcohol left in the tubes wouldn't have frozen, and in the cold weather it would take a while to evaporate. It might be possible to narrow down the time frame within which the man was killed by finding out when Trevelyan Buggins had filled his last vinegar jug. Minerva Mink ought to be able to tell that, though what use could be made of the information remained to be seen.

Maybe they should have waded into the bureaucratic morass at the Veterans Administration or wherever and tried to find out if there'd ever been any clarification of Bainbridge Buggins's missing-in-action status. If there had, though, surely the family would have been notified and Grace Porble would have known. Her theory that Bainbridge had deserted made plenty of sense in view of what Hesperus Hudson had said about his old pal; Bain wouldn't have bothered to leave a forwarding address with his commanding officer. He'd have fixed himself up with a new identity first crack off the bat. From the sound of him, he'd have skinned some victim's hands to provide himself with a different set of fingerprints if he took the notion. Whether or not they were Trevelyan's legal begets, those Buggins twins must have been a pair of first-class bastards.

Jane was climbing his pantleg, demanding her share of the fried bacon. Shandy shoved the Buggins boys to the back of his mind and buckled down to the business at hand.

Chapter 18

"**E**xcellent, darling." Helen set down her empty cup. "Now I'm afraid I've got to run. You can't imagine how much administrative work there is to running that library. I do not see how Thorkjeld manages to keep this whole college going and stay on top of everything the way he does. Right now he's neck-deep in revamping the dairy-management curriculum, working with the architect on plans for the new wing on Lower West dorm, trying to squeeze a few more thousand dollars out of the endowment fund for that bunch of seniors who came up with a great plan for a cooperative orchard and haven't the capital to start it with, and about twenty more projects. And that doesn't count the usual day-to-day stuff like breaking the news to a freshman girl that her pet iguana died back in Tuscaloosa because her parents hadn't the guts to tell her themselves. She took it hard, poor kid."

"Great balls of fire, you know more about what's happening around campus than I've found out in the past twenty years," said Shandy.

"Information is a librarian's business, dear. Besides, Sieglinde stopped in here last evening, too. She's awfully grateful to you for taking this Oozak's Pond business off Thorkjeld's hands while he's so swamped himself. She's been keeping him well stoked with herring to help him over the hump, she says, but there's a limit to what even herring can do. By the way, maybe you'd better pick up some herring if you're near the fish market today."

"I don't know what I'm going to be near. The brink, I'd say offhand."

After Helen left, Shandy sat brooding over his eggy plate. At last he got up, cleared away the dishes, and went to put on one of his elderly but still good gray worsted suits. He couldn't see any special reason why he should attend the Buggins funeral, but neither did he see a reason not to. Besides, he was curious to be on hand if Bracebridge Buggins turned up alive and litigious. The more he heard about the wily twin, the firmer his conviction became that this asinine lawsuit had a strong flavor of Bracebridge about it.

Bracebridge did not come, though, and nobody was acting as if he'd been expected. Hesperus Hudson appeared, to Shandy's surprise, cleaned up and togged out in a fairly respectable outfit that most likely belonged to Zack. Hudson looked more genuinely crestfallen than most of the other alleged mourners, as was no more than fitting in one whose life experiences had been so closely intertwined with Trevelyan's. No doubt he was grieving because nobody was left to run the still, but at least Hudson's was a genuine sorrow.

Marietta Woozle must have taken the morning off from the Pied Pica Press, either to pay her respects or to keep a sharp eye on her uncle. She was one of the more smartly turned out congregants in a bright blue coat and a white furry hat, with white boots and a red handbag.

Captain Flackley and his wife were there, too, both wearing Sherpa coats and subdued expressions. Shandy didn't see any soulful glances pass between Flackley and his dressy neighbor, but he'd hardly have expected to, under the present circumstances. Comparing Marietta Woozle to the attractive Yvette Flackley, Shandy found it hard to believe glances would pass under any circumstances and wondered why he'd thought they might.

Miss Minerva Mink was there, but not with her bingo

chauffeuse. One of the Minks must have gone out and got her. She was sitting with the family, as was only right and proper, being Purvis's aunt and the former prop and mainstay of the deceased. As well as the possible inheritor of their property. Shandy wondered whether Trevelyan Buggins had ever got around to making a will. It would be a touching gesture if he'd left his still to Hesperus Hudson.

There was a pretty good crowd in the church. Shandy recognized several of the garden club ladies. Grace Porble was not among them. She was up front with Sephy and the Minks, looking as if she'd been dragged backward through a knothole but keeping a brave face in front of the congregation.

At least Porble had a cast-iron excuse not to come with her. He hated getting dragged to any sort of ceremony, and he certainly entertained no mellow feelings toward the Bugginses even if he hadn't, as Harry Goulson so delicately put it, effected their demise.

Chief Ottermole wasn't here, of course. Shandy hadn't expected him to be. Neither was Edna Mae. She was probably home crocheting a bedspread for the roll-away cot. Silvester Lomax's wife was present and no doubt Clarence's as well, though Shandy didn't know the latter on sight. Betsy Lomax was also on deck in her respectable black coat with the muskrat collar and cuffs she'd inherited from an aunt who'd married the druggist over in Hoddersville and lived pretty high on the hog. From the back row came an occasional muffled sneeze and a frequent sniffle that indicated Cronkite Swope was back on the job.

Mike Woozle's inamorata not only hadn't come with Miss Mink, she evidently hadn't come at all. Shandy looked in vain for the red wig and the ratty fake fur. Maybe Marietta had persuaded Flo to stay away, or maybe Flo simply hadn't got up in time. Half past eight was pretty early for a funeral but convenient for those who wished to show their sympathy and still get their day's work done. Therefore, it was a favored time in Balaclava Junction, though possibly not among the jet set out at the Seven Forks. Would Flo have wound up at the Dirty Duck last evening? Probably not, since Mike's brother hung out there, but Shandy was inclined to think she'd wound up somewhere other than Marietta Woozle's kitchen. Well, all flesh was as grass, as the minister was even now reminding his hearers, and grass needed moisture to thrive. Shandy shifted uncomfortably on the oaken pew seat and wondered again what he was here for.

The service was a fairly lengthy one, not that the minister could find a great deal to say about Mr. and Mrs. Buggins by way of a eulogy. He padded out the rite with several of the old gospel hymns the Bugginses were reputed to have sung together over the years. That was all right, Shandy liked to sing hymns. Besides, they gave him a chance to stand up and stretch a bit in an unobtrusive way. He was pleasantly surprised to hear Hesperus Hudson singing, too, and deeply touched by the fervor Hudson put into the one about drinking at a fountain that never would run dry. But it was during "Rock of Ages" that Shandy got his revelation.

From then on, he was on pins and needles, but the service finished at last, as all things must. Then he had to stand waiting while the mourners filed out behind the now closed double casket, which just about squeaked through the narrow aisle with Harry Goulson steering and two of Arabella's cousins who helped out sometimes propelling from behind.

Persephone Mink had her handkerchief out, dabbing at her cheeks. Purvis Mink was looking embarrassed, as a husband naturally would, and keeping a hand on his wife's shoulder in a reckless public display of affectionate concern. Grace Porble was staring straight ahead of her, walking like an automaton. Miss Mink was looking prim and self-righteous. The rest were just looking tired and slightly relieved.

Since Shandy had chosen to sit far back in the church, he was among the last to leave, he and the sniffling Swope. "You going to the cemetery, Professor?" the reporter asked, punctuating his question with a sneeze.

"*Gesundheit*," said Shandy. "No, I'm not. Don't let me detain you."

"Oh, I'm not going, either. Funerals are Arabella's department. I was just wondering what new developments have arisen in the murder case."

"I had a feeling you might be. As of now, we're still more or less where we were."

"But, gosh, Professor, you're not going to leave Dr. Porble languishing in the coop, are you?"

"Is he languishing? I haven't been to see him yet today."

"Neither have I, but why wouldn't he be? I'd languish. You'd languish. Wouldn't you?"

"Swope, if it's your intention to get off a lot of slop about 'Librarian Languishes in Lockup—'"

"For cry-eye, Professor, what do you take me for?" yelped the virus-ridden journalist. "I haven't written one word about Dr. Porble getting arrested, and I don't intend to unless I'm driven to it. Fred Ottermole said he'd break my neck if I did, and I wouldn't, anyway."

"What? You mean Ottermole's passing up a chance to get his picture with a brand-new haircut in the *Fane and Pennon*, and you're going along with him?"

"Well, sure. Why not? You've cooperated with us often enough. See, Fred figured he had to take some action on Dr. Porble in the face of the evidence, but he doesn't really believe Dr. Porble's guilty, so Fred's kind of sitting on him till you come up with the real murderer. That way, Fred figures he won't come out looking like a schnook."

"Like a what?"

"A schnook. Kind of a dumb jerk who gets himself into stupid situations."

"M'yes, that would seem to be the *mot juste*. I must say, I'm filled with admiration and gratitude at your mutual restraint. Perhaps we might go together and check on Dr. Porble's present state of languishment. I have something to discuss with Ottermole, anyway. Do you have your camera with you, by the way?"

"Well, not exactly with me, no. I didn't think the minister would want me to bring it into the church. But it's in the trunk of the press car. You don't mean you want me to take a picture of Dr. Porble in the lockup, after all?"

"I do not, and I shouldn't advise you to get any second thoughts on the matter yourself, unless you plan on involving the *Fane and Pennon* in a lawsuit. I merely want to know if the camera will be ready to hand when and if it's needed."

"Oh. Sure thing, Professor. All gassed up and rarin' to go. Plenty of film, plenty of flashbulbs. Just point me in the right direction and tell me when to shoot. Hey, I think my cold's gone."

"Divine intervention, perhaps. Let's go, Swope."

They got themselves out of the push in the vestibule just in time to see Grace Porble cast an anguished glance in the direction of the police station before she got into one of the black limousines that were thrown in at no extra charge as part of Goulson's friendly service to friends and neighbors. Poor woman, she must be going through a terrible time. Well, with any luck, she'd be out of the Slough of Despond pretty soon.

In deference to Swope's convalescent status, they rode in the press car to the police station, though this was only a matter of backing up a hundred feet or so and pulling into a different parking spot. Inside, they found Dr. Porble was not languishing in the lockup. On the contrary, he was sitting at Chief Ottermole's desk with Edmund on his lap, a cup of coffee at his elbow, and a great many file folders sorted into piles in front of him.

"Morning, Peter," he said rather absently, with his eyes on the files.

"Hi, Phil," Shandy replied. "Been promoted to trusty?"

"I'm just trying to organize a more efficient filing system so Ottermole won't get stuck with so much unnecessary paperwork. It's utterly ridiculous the way this town over-works its grossly underpaid employees. I'm going to have something to say about the matter at town meeting, I can tell you."

"You have my wholehearted approval and support. Where's the chief?"

"Ottermole got called out on a robbery. Somebody's broken into the turkey-farm kitchen and stolen six turkey pies."

"Great Scott, he's not going to arrest a fox?"

"A fox wouldn't have swiped six plastic knives and forks to eat the pies with. Ottermole pounced on that clue right away. He just phoned in to say he's traced the miscreant through tracks in the snow and will be effecting a collar, so would I kindly hide the comic books under the cot mattress to make the lockup look more official?"

"Comic books?"

"Yes, his boys insisted on bringing them down for me to read when they found out I'm a librarian. They had them all arranged in alphabetical order. Refreshing to find there are still youngsters around who know their ABC's. I hadn't seen Superman for something like forty-five years. He doesn't seem to have changed a great deal, though I'll admit my memory's unclear on the details. How's Helen making out at the library?"

"She's coping but none too happy about having to. Administration's not her thing. She'll be relieved to get back to the Buggins Collection."

"No accounting for tastes," Porble grunted. "You haven't come to get me out of here, by any chance?"

"Not just now. Soon, I hope."

"Well, stall it off for another hour or two if you can. I hate to leave a job undone. Ah, here's Ottermole. Where's your prisoner, Chief?"

"Aw, he was just some poor bastard in a busted-down van with a wife an' two little kids. He got laid off from his job at a factory up in New Hampshire. His unemployment run out, an' they got evicted from their place, so they parked their stuff in somebody's garage and started out to see if he could find work down here. But he ain't had no luck, an' they hadn't eaten for two days, so what the hell? I talked Jack Pointer into givin' the guy a job delousin' turkey coops. It ain't much, but they'll eat. We couldn't squeeze 'em all in here, anyways. How you comin', Doc?"

"Quite well. I find it rather relaxing, actually."

"I don't. Hi, Professor. Hey, Cronk, what are you doin' here? You know what I told you about keepin' this out o' the paper."

"Don't worry, Ottermole," said Shandy. "Swope's, er, with me. I want you to swear us both in as your deputies, and, Phil, I want you to witness the swearing-in. I assume there's no legal problem about that, Ottermole, since Porble hasn't been formally arrested."

"What do you mean arrested?" Ottermole sounded hurt. "Doc's just here to reorganize the files while bein' held in protective custody as a material witness."

Witness to what? Shandy didn't ask. He merely stood waiting while the chief flapped around trying to make up his mind as to the correct procedure for swearing in a deputy. He'd sworn both Shandy and Swope in before, as a matter of fact, by saying something like "Okay, you guys are deputies. Let's go." This time, however, Ottermole naturally wanted to put on a good show in front of his distinguished temporary assistant.

In fact, he managed quite nicely, even allowing Cronkite Swope to take a picture of him swearing in Professor Shandy, provided he keep Dr. Porble well out of camera range. "Makes it more official," he explained. "Now, Cronk, I'll swear you in an' the professor can take one of us."

Shandy fretted a bit at this unnecessary delay, but reason told him there was no need to rush off. If his hunch was correct, his quarry had no intention of going anywhere in a hurry, and Ottermole had earned the right to spread his tail feathers. He took the picture.

"And lastly, Ottermole, I want you to make me out a search warrant."

"Sure, Professor, anything you say. Where are you plannin' to search?"

Shandy told him. Porble's eyebrows went up, but he said nothing and went on with his methodical checking of the files, while the police chief filled out the warrant.

"Okay, Professor, that ought to do it. You want me to go with you?"

"On the contrary, I particularly do not want you to go with me," Shandy answered. "No offense, Ottermole, but right now I have nothing whatever to work on except a funny feeling. Taking somebody along who, er, smacks of officialdom could ruin any possible chance I might have of finding out whether I'm barking up the right tree. Would I need another warrant to arrest somebody, by the way?"

"Nah, just bring 'em in. We'll get Doc here to handle the paperwork. Jeez, I hope you don't catch the real killer before we get them files straightened out."

"Dr. Porble has already expressed a similar wish. Speaking for myself, I'd like to wrap things up as quickly as possible and get my wife back. She's declared a moratorium on domesticity for the duration. Swope, you're welcome to come if you care to."

"Wouldn't miss it, Professor. Where are we going?"

"First to my house."

That clearly wasn't the sort of *Blazing Saddles* takeoff Swope had envisioned, but he went cheerfully enough and entertained Jane Austen with a wad of paper on a string while Shandy spent a long time and no doubt a great deal of money making long-distance phone calls.

"All right, Swope. Bainbridge Buggins is still officially missing in action. The shipping line doesn't know where Boatwright Buggins is. Trowbridge has been off on a geological field trip for the past three weeks, and Bracebridge hasn't been seen at the Wayfarers' Rest since 1972. Now I think I know where we're heading. Let's put the show on the road."

Chapter 19

They'd left the press car sitting out on the drive in defiance of Crescent protocol. Mirelle Feldster was out on her front steps next door, ready to give them an earful, but Shandy only gave her a nod and climbed in beside Swope.

"Where to, Professor?"

"Head for the Seven Forks," Shandy told him, "and thank God it's you driving instead of me. I feel as if I've worn a groove in the road out there."

"Are we going back to the Buggins place?"

"Eventually. First we stop at the Dirty Duck."

"For Pete's sake, why?"

"To see if we can collect Hesperus Hudson without having to face his niece. You wouldn't be safe a minute in that woman's clutches."

"Is she the one in the white boots who brought him to the funeral?"

"She is."

"Then I guess I wouldn't." Cronkite didn't sound flattered, only scared. "I've run into a couple like her going around doing interviews on should the dog license be extended to cats and other vital issues of the day. There was one woman who—well, I finally had to make believe I'd had the mumps at a delicate age. So she gave me the name of some friend of hers who thinks he's a faith healer like that guy in the Philippines with the rusty jackknife and told me to come back when I was cured. What I do now is,

I stay out on the doorstep. The important thing about being a journalist is learning to keep clear of big, soft sofas. I wrote to the Famous Journalists' Correspondence School about putting it in the curriculum, but I sort of don't think they will."

"M'well, perhaps they feel some things have to be learned by experience," said Shandy. "Aha, we're right on the button. Here he comes now."

Hesperus Hudson was in fact just emerging from the woods. Marietta must have known better than to let him escape in those respectable clothes, as he was now clad in the horrible garments he'd been wearing last night and no doubt for many nights before that. The bath hadn't quite worn off, and he hadn't had a chance to let his whiskers grow back, but time would take care of that. As he steered toward the Dirty Duck, his face wore an expression of happy anticipation. When Shandy got out of the car and walked over to him, it changed.

"I know you."

"I know you, too, Mr. Hudson," Shandy replied affably. "I enjoyed your singing in church this morning."

"Huh? You tryin' to start somethin'?"

Surprisingly, Hudson's right hand whipped out of his pocket equipped with a tarnished but serviceable set of brass knuckles.

"Very impressive," said Shandy. "Are those the same ones you laid Bracebridge Buggins's chin open with?"

"I didn't kill 'im!"

"I never said you did. How would you like to make ten dollars?"

"I already got ten dollars. What I'd like is for you to get the hell out o' my way so's I can go in here an' spend it."

"But then that ten dollars will be gone and you'll be thirsty again. If you had another ten, you could stay drunk longer."

"Put not the cup to thy brother's lips." Hudson was full of surprises today.

"I'm not putting any cup to your lips," Shandy replied testily.

"You damn well better hadn't try. I'd rather have it straight from the bottle any day. Okay, let's have the ten."

"I didn't say I was going to give it to you outright. You'll have to earn it."

"I knew there was goin' to be a catch somewheres. Doin' what?"

"Merely taking my friend and myself to see Trevelyan Buggins's still."

"What for? There ain't nothin' left in it. I already looked."

"I know, but I want to look for myself. Last night, as you may or may not recall, you told me a remarkable story."

"Who, me?"

"Yes, you." How did they keep getting into this Abbott and Costello cross talk? "You said you'd gone to the still house and found a man whom you took to be Bracebridge Buggins disguised as Henry Wadsworth Longfellow lying there dead."

"What if I did? No law against findin' a stiff, is there? You tryin' to make out I killed 'im?"

"By no means, Mr. Hudson. I'm extremely grateful to you for coming forth with the information. That's why I gave you the ten last night."

"You gimme that ten, too?"

"I certainly did. Where did you think you got it?"

"I thought maybe it was the tooth fairy."

"You're a card, Mr. Buggins. A deuce or a trey, perhaps. How far is the still house from here?"

"It's back there."

He waved an arm pretty much as he'd done last night. Shandy grabbed at the shreds of his temper.

"Precisely where back there? Is this the shortest way in,

or would we make better time going around by First Fork?"

"Oh, yeah, First Fork would be quicker. You gonna gimme a ride?"

"If you want one, sure," said Cronkite Swope. "Pile in."

"But I was plannin' to get drunk."

"Here," said Shandy, who'd anticipated some such objection and come equipped to deal with it. "Drink this."

The pocket flask he'd brought along only held about one stiff drink, but he didn't want Hudson to have more than enough to get his tonsils in working order before their mission was completed.

At least it was enough to get him into the car and begin shouting thoroughly garbled directions. Despite his help, they managed to get the car stashed under some overhanging evergreens and find the well-trampled path that led to the small, weathered board shack. There was another path leading to it from the Second Fork side.

"I done that," Hudson told them with some pride. "Mostly, anyways."

"Why? Do other people come here, too?" Shandy asked him.

"I guess likely. Kids lookin' for a quiet place to do what comes natural, hunters takin' a rest an' gettin' warm. Build up a little fire under the still there an' you can get the place hot in a few minutes. Cut up a rabbit an' roast it if you can get one. Or a grouse. Grouse is good eatin'. You could bring in a sack o' rotten potatoes an' brew yourself up a little somethin' to drink with it, I s'pose, if you'd a mind to."

"Have you done that yourself, Mr. Hudson?"

"Not me. Too much like work." Disregarding the rusty padlock hanging from the hasp, Hudson picked the screws from the rotted-out holes behind the hinges and swung the door open from the wrong side. "Make yourselves to home."

The shack did in fact have a slight air of hominess about it. Since old Buggins had spent so much of his life there, tending his still, he'd naturally have wanted to add a few creature comforts. There was an old porch rocker with its rush seat broken through and a grimy brown plush sofa pillow plugging up the hole. On the ledge beside it were several rusty tobacco tins, a pipe with the stem almost bitten through, a fancy ashtray, and a stack of assorted magazines. Shandy was mildly intrigued to see a few copies of *Collier's Weekly* among them. He could just about remember his own father sitting on the front porch they'd once had, in a rocking chair like this one, reading *Collier's Weekly*.

This was hardly the time or the place for childhood reminiscences. "How was the body lying, Mr. Hudson?" he asked.

"Down," said his star witness promptly. "Ever see anybody layin' up?"

"A pithy observation," snarled Shandy. "Was it here?"

He pointed to the floor beside the rocking chair, which was about the only place a grown man could have been stretched out to full length. The corners were filled with stacks of firewood and empty vinegar jugs, the middle of the little room was occupied by the fieldstone chimney and the square firebox on which sat the big, closed pot with the copper condensing coil sprouting out of its lid. The coil ended above a plastic bucket that had once held a compound for cleaning floors. Shandy wondered if Buggins had used the stuff to enhance the flavor of his hell-brew.

"Yup," Hudson was saying. "He was layin' right there where you're pointin'. His head was up against the rocker, an' his feet was pointin' towards the door. He looked real peaceful, like he'd just passed out from the booze, 'cept his eyes were starin' an' his mouth was open."

Swope was making frantic scribbles on a wad of copy paper. "Hey, Professor, can I print this?"

"I don't see why not. We should have the whole story before too many more hours have passed. Maybe you'd like to take a—ah!"

Shandy stepped gingerly across the plank floor and pointed to a few whitish long hairs caught under a splinter. "See those? I'll bet you dollars to doughnuts they're from that fake beard the dead man was wearing."

He began crawling around the planks, snagging the knees of his own trousers more than once. "And here's a black thread, and another. If there are corresponding pulls on the back of that old coat, I think we can call them conclusive proof that the body was parked here after the man was killed, just as Hudson testifies. It's quite conceivable he was actually murdered here. Did you happen to notice a small stab wound in the back of his neck when you moved him, Hudson?"

"Huh? He wasn't bleedin'."

"No, I expect he wouldn't have been. It was only a puncture, really. From an ice pick or something of the sort."

"Brace always liked ice in 'is drinks," said Hudson. "We'd sneak into the Flackleys' icehouse an' hack off a piece an' bring it here so's he could fix his like he wanted it."

"I thought you said you drank it hot from the still with a reed for a straw," said Shandy.

"That was me an' Bain. Bain didn't give a damn, an' neither did I. Brace was the fussy one. He'd even wipe off the sawdust before he put the ice in 'is cup. He had this little collapsin' cup that he carried around in 'is pocket."

"Did he carry an ice pick, too?" Shandy asked.

"Nope. Didn't have to. There was always one in the icehouse."

"I see. Would the icehouse be still standing, by any chance?"

"Prob'ly. The Flackleys was always great ones for keepin' things like they used to be."

"But they don't cut ice any more, do they?"

Hudson shrugged. "What for?"

"Still, they'd leave the ice pick in the icehouse?"

"How the hell do I know? Ask them, why don't you?"

"Do you think the Flackleys' ice pick was the murder weapon, Professor?" asked Swope.

"I'm not going to think anything until I know for sure whether or not the Flackleys still have an ice pick," Shandy said rather irritably. "If you want to be helpful, Swope, why don't you snap a picture of me taking samples of these threads from the floor? It's not for publication, just for evidence."

"I could take one for you and one for the paper, too."

"All right, but let's get on with it. We're not through yet, you know."

"Why? What else do we have to do?"

"Catch the murderer, among other things. Mr. Hudson, you've been extremely helpful. Here's your ten and another to go with it. Now Swope's going to drive you back to the Dirty Duck, and I'd be most grateful if you'd refrain from talking to anybody there about what's been happening here."

"Huh. Won't be anybody there to talk to, anyways, not this early in the day, 'cept that fat ol' slob Margery that tends bar till Jack comes in, an' she don't like me. She says I lower the tone o' the place."

"A feat few could accomplish," Shandy said politely. "Godspeed, Mr. Hudson. Swope, take that press card out of your windshield. Leave your car at the Dirty Duck and walk back through the woods if you think you can manage it without getting lost. I'm going on to the Buggins house. If you see a car in the driveway or any other sign of activity when you get there, don't try to come in. Stay out of sight, and be careful about making footprints in unbroken snow," he added, mindful of the turkey pie thief's providential capture. If Cronkite Swope fell into the wrong hands now, though, there'd be no happy ending for him.

"I get you, Professor," Swope answered. "Come on, Mr. Hudson."

Shandy left them and beelined it for the house, hoping he hadn't dallied too long. He'd taken it for granted Miss Mink would go to the cemetery and then to her nephew's house with the rest of the family, but he wouldn't put it past the old basket to develop a headache or a case of the pip and insist on being brought back to squat on her claim.

No, by George, she hadn't. Nobody was around, no car in the yard, no sign of life anywhere. Yet the door wasn't locked. That was a surprise. Shandy had come prepared for burglarious entry, sure Miss Mink would have battened down the hatches before she left for the funeral. Maybe she'd been too overcome with grief to bother, though she hadn't shown any sign of that at the church. Or maybe whoever picked her up had been in a hurry and flustered her into forgetting.

Anyway, the open door was a break for him. Shandy inched his way inside, making sure somebody was not, after all, sitting behind the drawn curtains, and went straight upstairs.

It was Trevelyan Buggins's den he aimed for first. Here, he found just about what he'd expected: a couple of rump-sprung armchairs with gaudy Dacron-filled comforters hanging over their backs, a middle-aged television set, a lot more old magazines, and the collected works of Corydon Buggins, bound in limp green suede and inscribed, "To my beloved nephew Knightsbridge Buggins on his eighteenth birthday."

That would have been Trevelyan's father, son of the Ichabod who'd established the family tradition of not amounting to much. Shandy picked up the book. It flopped open of itself to the page where Augustus

Buggins's appalling end was described, complete with a gloomy steel engraving of a darksome mere and a floating body. He wondered how much Knightsbridge had enjoyed reading about the awful demise of a cousin from the more successful branch of the family and whether Trevelyn had relished it, too.

Shandy put the book back where he'd found it, took down a cardboard file, and searched through it for possible revelations about the lawsuit. Trevelyan had prepared an inner folder grandly inscribed, "Documents pertaining to the Ichabod Buggins family lawsuit against Balaclava Agricultural College in the matter of Oozak's Pond," but there was nothing in it except a carbon copy of the same letter President Svenson had been so wroth to receive. He pawed around a little more, checked out the bedrooms, found nothing of interest, and went on to the attic.

The Bugginses were savers, no doubt about that. Here were enough copies of *Life*, *Look*, and *Liberty Magazine* to have stocked a newsstand back in the thirties. Here were gift boxes without any presents in them, candy boxes with no candy, empty bags, empty baskets, empty relics of empty lives. And here were old clothes enough to start a moth farm, empty of moths. They'd all been carefully preserved with naphtha flakes in the pockets and once-white sheets or cleaners' bags around them. Shandy had almost forgotten that cleaners' bags used to be made of shiny paper. These were dusty, yellowed, brittle with age. And one was freshly torn.

Shandy sneaked across the grimy plank floor and tore it some more. Here it was, the thing he'd come looking for, proof of where the antique suit had been taken from and why it had to go. Now he knew the name of the man he'd fished out of Oozak's Pond.

Chapter 20

Drat it, where was Swope? Shandy wanted a photograph of what he'd discovered, showing the place where it had been hanging. And what was that small noise from below him? It sounded like a window being inched open.

Shandy remembered that there'd been a tree badly in need of trimming just outside the den window, with one bough that rubbed right up against the house. Moving as softly as he could, careful not to step on any board that looked creaky, he got down the worn, steep attic stairs and crept along the hall. By some carpenter's vagary, the door to the den opened out instead of into the room and provided a convenient screen. Peeking through the crack, he could see a bright new green rubber sole, followed by the rest of a Maine hunting boot poking in through the window.

He was around the door in a flash. "Swope, why in perdition couldn't you use the door?"

The young newspaperman grinned. "Windows are kind of a habit of mine. How do you think I got away from my mother this morning? I figured Mr. Buggins never got around to putting any locks upstairs. What's happening, Professor?"

"Come on."

Shandy rushed him up to the attic, ripped away what was left of the cleaners' bag, and said, "Shoot."

"Sure, if you say so. But it's just somebody's—"

"Shh!"

Something was happening downstairs. They could hear a creak, then another creak, then a whole series of creaks in steady rhythm. Then a whiff of pipe smoke drifted up the narrow stairwell.

Great balls of fire, Shandy thought, was Trevelyan Buggins back from the funeral with that detoxified pipe in his waxwork hand, having one final puff in the old rocking chair before he settled down beside his wife for their last, long sleep? On the whole, Shandy didn't think so. He was remembering his second visit to Miss Minerva Mink. He'd smelled pipe smoke that night, too, and old man Buggins was already dead. Was it possible the elderly housekeeper had a gentleman friend?

"I'm going down," Shandy mouthed to Swope. "You stay here and guard the evidence. If anybody comes up here, deck him. And for God's sake, don't sneeze."

Swope was already pressing a finger frantically against his upper lip. The dust must be getting to those inflamed nasal passages. He nodded like a good soldier, and Shandy went.

The stairs would have been a risk, but luckily for Shandy, a diversion occurred at the right moment. A car drove into the yard, and he could hear Minerva Mink telling somebody not to bother coming in with her, she just needed to be alone for a while. He lay belly-bumper on the once-varnished banister, prayed it was less rickety than it felt, and slid down without a sound. By the time she'd got herself into the kitchen, he was in the cheerless front parlor with his eye to the keyhole.

She was taking off her coat and hat, saying, "Whew, I'm glad that's over."

"Got 'em both nicely planted, eh?" The other voice, as Shandy had expected, was Flo's.

"That's a fine way to talk, I must say." The words might be chiding, but Miss Mink's voice was not. Shandy nodded to himself. His hunch was working out just fine. "What's that you're drinking?" she was asking now.

"What is there to drink around here? Here's to the old man. May he stew forever in his own juice!"

That didn't go down too well with Miss Mink. "I hope you didn't get hold of the wrong bottle."

"Damn the fear of it, dearie. You only put the poison into the opened jug, didn't you?"

"I did precisely what you told me to. I didn't know what that stuff was. You needn't go at me as I were a murderess."

"But that's exactly what you are, Minerva my love."

"And what are you? At least I didn't take a rusty old ice pick and—"

"Now, Minnie, don't go getting all haired up. We're partners, remember."

"And I get my equal share, don't you forget."

"You sure do, sweetheart. Come on, relax. Have a drink."

"Thanks, I'll have this one you just drank from. Go pour yourself another."

"Atta girl, Min! Sharp as a tack and a damn sight better-looking. First time I laid eyes on you, I knew you were the woman I'd been after all my life."

"How many others have you said that to? And when are you going to quit wearing those silly clothes?"

"In about half an hour. I just dropped in to say good-bye. Mike's given me the boot because he's formed a meaningful relationship with the warden, and I'm going out to commit suicide. Or maybe I'll just fade away sadly into the sunset. I haven't quite decided yet. For a suicide, I'd need a female corpse about five foot ten with false teeth, and that might be tough to come by."

"I know where you can get one, not far off."

"Now, Minnie, that's not a bit nice. She's come in very

handy, and we may need her again. Anyway, she doesn't have false teeth."

"Why should that stop you? You could pull them out, the way you did with—"

"We weren't going to talk about that, remember?"

Flo was up out of the rocking chair, getting another drink. Through the keyhole Shandy could see Miss Mink's partner crossing over to the cupboard. He had a clear view of the hands that had always been kept covered and of the head that wasn't wearing a wig. Without all that wild red hair obscuring them, the eyes showed up as a strange, opaque darkish gray, like slate.

"Here's to us, Min." Flo was drunk enough to be euphoric. "Three down and none to go, unless Sephy and that tin soldier she's married to start giving us trouble. How's darling Gracie?"

"Terribly upset, naturally."

"Glad to hear it. Starched-up little bitch."

"She's hardly little anymore. She's as tall as—don't you want to hear about the funeral?"

"No, I want to hear about Grace. Is she as tall as I am?"

"No, not nearly." Miss Mink sounded frightened. "And she's much slighter built."

"Too bad. All right, so who else was at the funeral?"

"All the gawkers in town, as you might expect. Your lady friend brought that drunken old uncle of hers."

"Hesp Hudson? No kidding! How did he act?"

"Reasonably sober, for a change. Of course, the way he bellowed out the hymns, you could hear him all over the church. I thought my eardrums were going to burst."

"Hesp Hudson singing hymns? That's a hot one!"

Flo was cracking up, practically falling off the rocking chair. Shandy wished the keyhole were more strategically placed. Then he leaped back like a scalded rabbit. Flo was up and heading for the parlor.

"Come on, Min, let's us sing a hymn. You can play the organ, can't you?"

"It's making a mockery."

"Mockery, hell. Think how respectable we'll sound when the neighbors come over with the pies. Chintzy bastards, why haven't they?"

"There's a nice cake Mrs. Flackley brought, if you want some."

"No, I don't want any of nice Mrs. Flackley's nice cake," Flo answered in a squeaky, mincing voice. "Here, let's both have another hair of the woof-woof to oil up the jolly old choobs, as we say in Liverpool, and away we go."

Luckily, there was another door to the parlor. Shandy was out in the stairwell trying to look like a grandfather's clock by the time Minerva Mink got her feet on the treadles and her hands on the keys of the pump organ. Doors in old houses never stay open unless you put a brick in front of them, so he was able to shut himself off from the singers without any fuss.

"Washed in the booze, by the spirits healed." Flo's rendition of the rousing old gospel song was hardly respectable, but Trevelyan Buggins's last batch was certainly an efficacious lubricant for the bronchii. Miss Mink must be well into the spirits, too, by this time. She was pulling out the loud stops and pumping for all she was worth. Under cover of the racket they were making, Shandy dared to reach for the telephone, make a tent of his overcoat to muffle the sound, and dial. This entailed squatting down so he could grip the instrument between his knees, cradling the receiver somewhat painfully between his chin and shoulder, holding his tiny pocket flashlight in a most peculiar way with most of his right-hand fingers while leaving the index finger free to dial with, and using the other hand to keep the coat in place, but he persevered and overcame. He even got the right number.

"Ottermole," he whispered, "I'm at the Buggins place on First Fork. Get out here as quick as you can. Bring Porble. Use his car; don't trust that wreck of yours. She's there, too? Good. Let her come."

They were still yowling like a pair of banshees on the other side of the door, so now that he'd got the knack, Shandy risked another call. He waited awhile, half-smothered in melton cloth, and made a third. Then he put the phone back and waited some more.

Marietta Woozle, last to be called, was the first to arrive. She'd taken longer than one might expect to cover so short a distance, though. Shandy had guessed she wouldn't go on to work after the funeral. Now he deduced she'd slipped into something comfortable, expecting to be the visited rather than the visitor, and had had to get dressed again. She was got up like a firecracker and acting the part.

"What the hell's going on here?" she yelled as she hurled open the door, driving the knob through the wall behind it, from the sound of the crash. "I could hear you all the way up the road. You slaughtering a hog or something?"

"Oh, hello, Marietta, darling." That was the person called Flo. "What brings you here? I thought we had other plans."

"So did I, you bastard."

"Now, sweetie, don't get sore. Minerva and I were just having a little religious service of our own, since I couldn't very well pay my respects in public. Pull up a chair, and join the party. Let me fix you a drink."

"Not for me, lover. I know the kind of drinks you two fix. Listen here, you creep—"

Marietta's own decibel rate had been rising steadily. Miss Mink took umbrage, having a bit of trouble with her sibilants.

"May I remind you this is a house of mourning?"

"Sure, go ahead and remind me. Try it with your teeth in next time."

"What did I tell you?" Miss Mink demanded, apparently of her fellow songster.

"Yeah, what did she tell you?" shouted Marietta. "I'll tell you what she told you. She told you to kill me, didn't she? You're planning to fake a suicide, and you want me for the corpse. You're going to pull out all my teeth so I can't be identified, just like you did—"

"Shut up!" Shandy could hear the slap. "Where did you hear that?"

"You ever hit me again, buster, and it'll be the last time you ever hit anybody. Never mind where I heard it. It's the truth, isn't it?"

"Of course it's not the truth. Who told you?"

"What's that to you?"

"If somebody's telling lies about me, I want to know. Besides, we only—"

"Said it a few minutes ago. I know."

"So you've been sneaking around listening outside the house, have you? That's a hell of a note." Flo's voice dropped to a gentle wheedle. "Honey, don't you trust me?"

"Sure, like a rattlesnake trusts a cobra. So you admit you said it."

"I'm not admitting anything. Look, baby, you know the plan. I have to get the Flo character out of the neighborhood in a way that won't start the Goddamn neighbors yapping about what happened to me so that I can come back as my real self."

"Whoever the hell that is."

"God, you're cute. That's what I love about you, baby. So anyway, Min and I were sort of kidding around about the best way to get me out of here, and I made a dumb joke about how I could fake a suicide if I had a dummy to put in my place."

"And I'm supposed to be the dummy. Thanks a bunch."

"Look, your name was never mentioned. Minerva said there was somebody handy who'd be about the right size, that's all. Maybe she's just a weensy bit jealous or something."

"That old bag of bones? Jesus, don't tell me you've been giving it to her, too?"

"If you think I'm going to stay in the same room with that trollop," Miss Mink began to shriek.

"Wait a minute! Wait a minute," yelled the person called Flo. "Look, we're all in this together, aren't we? What are you putting me in the middle for? I promised you I'd see you both got your cut, didn't I? I told you I'd cover up for you no matter what you did. So, okay, when Minerva put the carbon tet in the old folks' bedtime bottle—"

"I didn't know it would kill them! I only did what you told me to."

"Sure you did, sweetheart. Not that a jury would ever believe you. Look, you did us all a big favor. Marietta appreciates it as much as I do. Don't you, Marietta, baby? It's just like when you got a little bit impetuous with that ice pick out in the still house."

"Why, you lousy rat fink! Okay, lover. I took the ice pick from the icehouse at Forgery Point the same night I got the carbon tet from the shed, like you told me to. And I wore gloves, which you didn't tell me to because you were hoping I wouldn't think of that myself. And I handed the pick to you by the point, and you took the handle with your bare hand because you're not so Goddamn smart as you think you are. And after you'd rammed it into his neck and pulled it out and threw it in the corner behind the still, I went and got it back."

"The hell you did! When?"

"When you went back in the house to get the suit, that's when. And I picked it up real careful and wrapped it in some tissues and stowed it in my pocket because I'm a firm believer in carrying insurance, lover. And I've got it hidden with your fingerprints on it in a place you'd never find in a million years. But the cops will, because I've taken care of that little detail, too. So don't give me that impetuous crap, lover."

"Jesus, Marietta—"

"And furthermore, I saw where you threw those pliers you pulled his teeth out with, and I saw you throw the teeth, too. And I remember exactly where they landed because I've got a photographic memory, and I never forget a thing, as you damned well know."

"Marietta, you wouldn't!"

"Wouldn't turn you in and testify against you? Don't kid yourself, lover. If you ever try to get funny with me again, you're dead. Now, let's talk sense for a change."

"Yes, let's," said Miss Mink feebly.

Marietta was running the show now. "Never mind who did what. We've all got a hell of a lot invested in this deal, and we're going to pull it off. Don't sweat it, we're clean as a whistle so far. Okay, I had to stick my neck out with that lie about seeing Porble's car, but it worked, didn't it? He's in jail, isn't he?"

"Only in the lockup," Miss Mink corrected.

"Don't worry, we'll soon fix that. Look, we're golden. All we have to do is keep our teeth out of each other's throats and play it the way we planned it. Now I'm going home and forget I had that anonymous phone call. Flo, you're going into the general store with a big tale of woe about Mike giving you the air. Make it good. Buy a box of mouse poison or something."

"Thanks, sweetie."

"Any time, lover. So then you come whining to me after Zack gets home, and I drive you to the bus station with your own clothes in a suitcase."

"And how do I get back?"

"Call some of the family, dum-dum. Stage a big reunion scene, then say you don't want to put them out and since Minerva's here alone, you'll do them a big favor and stay with her. And you, Min, lie down and look pathetic till they come. God knows you can handle that."

"Wait a minute," said Flo. "What about that anonymous phone call?"

"And what if that Professor Shandy comes nosing around here again?" wailed Miss Mink. "I don't trust him an inch."

"Forget Shandy. He's most likely up at the college chewing his thumb and wondering what to do next."

Now was as good a time as any. Shandy opened the parlor door and stepped through. "Er, no. As a matter of fact, I'm here."

He raised his voice. "Come on down, Swope, ready to shoot!"

Chapter 21

"Don't shoot!" The person called Flo flung his hands in the air.

Marietta Woozle sneered. "My hero! Jesus, you even make Zack look good to me."

Cronkite Swope thundered down the stairs. "Who do you want shot, Professor?"

"All of them, if they so much as flicker an eyebrow," said Shandy ferociously. "Now, by the authority vested in me by Chief Ottermole of the Balaclava Junction Police Force, I declare you three to be under arrest on a charge of conspiracy to murder. There will be further charges, including the one about defrauding Balaclava Agricultural College of an undetermined sum of money, but I don't think it's necessary to go into all that just now. Deputy Swope, would you mind reading them their rights? I've forgotten to bring my reading glasses."

"This is illegal," cried Minerva Mink. "You had no right sneaking in here while my back was turned."

"As a matter of fact, we entered the house while you were at your nephew's," Shandy clarified, "and we did it legally. I have a search warrant here somewhere."

"But you had nothing to search for." She was a game old bird, at any rate.

"Yes we did. We sought it, and we found it. The jig, not to put too fine a point on the matter, is up. All is discovered, and you're headed for the bin. Mrs. Woozle, since you expressed some interest a while back in turning state's evidence, I think now would be the time to give that possibility your earnest consideration."

"Hey, Professor, here's the chief," yelled Swope.

"Good," said Shandy. "I thought I heard a couple of cars turning into the road a moment ago. That, quite candidly, is why I interrupted this interesting discussion when I did. I thought it would save a lot of fuss and bother if we could present our reinforcements with a *fait accompli*. You'd better hurry up and read the rights, Swope."

"Sure, Professor." Cronkite whipped through the printed sheet Ottermole had given without missing a comma. "Now can I shoot?"

"Go ahead."

"But we've surrendered!" Marietta was screaming when Swope's flashbulb went off.

"Sorry," he apologized, "I'm afraid I got you with your mouth open. Want me to try another shot?"

"Oh, Jesus, a photographer," she moaned. "Look, I don't have to be in the picture if I'm going to rat."

"I'm going to rat, too," said Miss Mink firmly.

"Rats do desert a sinking ship, you see, Mr. Buggins," said Shandy. "Hello, Ottermole. Here are your killers. Reading from left to right, Mrs. Marietta Woozle, Miss Minerva Mink, and Mr. Bracebridge Buggins."

"Bracebridge?" cried a voice from the back. There was quite a crowd in the house by now. "Are you sure that's not Bain, Professor?"

"Oh, hello, Goulson. I didn't expect to see you here."

"I just happened to drop in at the station as Fred and the Porbles were leaving. They told me to come along. You haven't identified the loved one, by any chance?"

"I'm working up to it, Goulson. Where's my wife?"

"With me." President Svenson bulled his way through the pack, towing Helen in his wake. "All three?"

"Not me," Marietta shrilled. "It was Min here who put the carbon tetrachloride in the vinegar jug."

"But I didn't know it was going to kill them," Miss Mink protested. "I only did it because he told me to."

"And his object, I expect," said Shandy, "was simply to reduce the number of people who stood to benefit from that lawsuit Mr. Buggins was so sure of winning. His parents went first, no doubt, because they were the easiest to get rid of."

"Wait a minute, Professor," Ottermole objected. "It was the guy in the pool who went first. If this guy's Brace-bridge—"

"He is. See, Goulson, there's that triangular scar under the jawbone you and I were looking for on the corpse last night. For your information, Ottermole, Hesperus Hudson has testified that he did that many years ago with a pair of brass knuckles formerly the property of Bainbridge Buggins."

"Then Bainbridge was the one in the pool, right?"

"Wrong. Bainbridge Buggins may conceivably still be alive somewhere, despite official government opinion to the contrary, but he appears to have played no part in this conspiracy. The man in the pool was not one of those who might have profited from the lawsuit. I'm sorry, Grace, but he's your brother Boatwright."

"Boatwright?" shouted Harry Goulson. "I knew Boat. Gosh, that's—I shouldn't say great, out of consideration for the bereaved, but at least Boatwright was somebody you could feel friendly toward."

"Boatwright?" Grace Porble was turning not to Shandy but to her own husband. "Phil, he can't be right, can he?"

"I'd find it hard to believe he made the identification without due cause," Dr. Porble replied. "Where's your evidence, Peter?"

"Hanging upstairs in the attic. We've found Captain Buggins's uniform.

"That's right," said Swope. "I took some shots of it, for evidence."

"Your brother's personal papers are still in the pockets," Shandy added. "I daresay Bracebridge thought they might come in handy for another of his impersonations. You see, Grace, I knew there must be some reason why the body in the pond had been dressed up in that old-fashioned suit. The false beard and the rocks in the pockets may have been meant as a final tribute to your brother's penchant for offbeat jokery, but they also gave us a lead toward identifying his killer."

"How was that, Peter?"

"Because they were part of a reenactment of the murder of one Augustus Buggins about eighty years ago."

"Balaclava's grandson," Helen put in.

"Thank you, my love. The crime was, er, poetically documented by Corydon Buggins. We found a copy of his collected poems upstairs in Trevelyan's den. The murderer would have had to know the story to have thought of the rocks. Since you've always shunned the Buggins Archive like the plague, Phil, you were an unlikely culprit."

"You didn't begin suspecting Helen, I hope?"

"Damn the fear of it. Bracebridge Buggins himself, in his, er, Flo persona, complained to me that Trevelyan Buggins was in the habit of telling the same stories over and over to anybody who'd listen. However, Trevelyan didn't get around much, so that limited the list of possible hearers to Grace, which was ridiculous; Persephone or Purvis Mink, who didn't seem likely; Miss Mink, Beatrice, or Trevelyan himself, none of whom would have had the strength to lug Boatwright around or the means of transportation to get him to Oozak's Pond; or someone else who'd spent a good deal of time in Trevelyan's company. Bracebridge had been gone for many years, but he had lived at home until he was drafted. No doubt he'd heard about Augustus's murder at his dear old daddy's knee lots of times, and it's the kind of yarn that might have had a special appeal to his, er, peculiar turn of mind."

"Damned peculiar," snorted the president. "Why the red dress?"

"He's been posing as a woman called Flo, purporting to be the lady friend of a local resident named Mike Woozle who's doing a, er, stretch."

"Eight years," Chief Ottermole amplified. "Robbery with assault. But cripes, Professor, Mike may have his little quirks, but he's not that kind of a guy."

"I doubt whether Mike Woozle has ever met Brace-bridge Buggins," said Shandy. "Bear in mind, however, that Marietta Woozle here happens to be Mike's sister-in-law. When Mike went to jail, he probably left his house and car keys with her and his brother. Precisely how she got to know Bracebridge will no doubt be revealed in her testimony once she gets down to ratting, but I expect we'll find he sought her acquaintance because she, er, had what it took."

"Watch it, buster," snarled Mrs. Woozle. "There's such a thing as defamation of character."

"Good try, Mrs. Woozle. I meant that having Mike's keys put you in a position to provide Bracebridge with housing and transportation. Pretending to be Mike's woman friend gave him an excuse to move in and take over. You were even the right size to lend him some of your old clothes. That's why the dress Bracebridge has on is red, President. If anybody recognized it, they'd think Mrs. Woozle was merely being charitable to her, er, potential sister-in-law. They were making plans a while ago for Bracebridge to leave town as Flo and come back as himself. I expected he'd then have identified Boatwright's body as his twin's and tried to convince us it was Bainbridge who'd mur-dered their parents and, quite possibly by then, their sister."

"But how could Brace make us think Bain had killed

Sephy if he was supposed to have been dead all this time?" cried Grace Porble. "That's impossible, Peter."

"Oh, no, he could have managed well enough. He'd only have had to choose some delayed-action method, like a booby trap Bainbridge would supposedly have set before he died. He might have got Miss Mink to give Persephone a jar of poisoned jelly, saying her mother had made it for her just before Mrs. Buggins died, or stuck a razor blade smeared with curare into the binding of her father's pet poetry book."

"Where would he get curare?"

"Who knows? I was only hypothesizing. There are plenty of less exotic tricks that might have worked."

Grace's brain didn't seem to be working just now, and no wonder. "And you're saying Brace killed my brother because he wanted the captain's uniform?"

"By no means. I'm saying your brother's clothes had to be changed because the captain's uniform would have immediately given away the fact that he was Boatwright and not Bainbridge. Bracebridge wanted his twin unquestionably dead, you see, so that when it came time to settle the lawsuit he expected to win, there wouldn't be any time wasted hunting for a missing heir."

"But how did Brace get hold of Boat?"

"My guess is that they'd been in contact off and on over the years. You may remember Bracebridge showed up in a naval officer's uniform shortly after the war. He may have borrowed it from your brother and gussied it up with some fake insignia, just for a joke. Boatwright would have gone alone with that; he must have had rather a freakish sense of humor, too, judging from the pair of back scratchers he sent you for a wedding present."

Grace was trying not to let anybody see she was crying. "I don't see why Boat couldn't have stopped by and said hello to me, if he was right here at First Fork."

"More than likely, he thought he was on his way to see

you. Bracebridge may have spun him a yarn that you were back living at First Fork, and he believed it. You said yourself you hadn't written to your brother for a long time."

"Why should I, when Boat never wrote back? And why would he think I was here?"

"Why shouldn't he, if his own cousin told him so?" That was Helen, being reasonable. "You'll believe anything if you've been out of touch for years and years. What if Bracebridge told him you'd had a fight with Phil and come home to the old folks? Or your house burned down and you needed a place to go in a hurry? Or First Fork had got to be fashionable and you'd moved out here to get away from the clods up around the college?"

"What clods?" demanded Thorkjeld Svenson.

"The ones Bracebridge got the curare from. I'm just showing how easy it would be. Do stop making faces, Thorkjeld. Can't you see Grace is upset?"

"Been upset myself, damn it. Anyway, the lawsuit's off. A murderer can't profit from his crime. He is a murderer, I hope."

"No question. Mrs. Woozle watched him stab Boatwright, and she's going to produce the weapon with his fingerprints on it. Aren't you, Mrs. Woozle?"

"You'd better believe it, lover. This bastard tried to pin that one on me, just as he stuck Min here for the other two."

"We were but pawns of his evil machinations," quavered Miss Mink.

"Yeah, sure," said Ottermole. "We'll get your statements down at the station. So Brace here was in touch with Boatwright all the time, eh?"

"I shouldn't say all the time," Shandy demurred. "They both led wandering lives, I'd assume they may have wandered in the same direction now and again. Bracebridge could have tracked his cousin down any time he cared to, merely by getting in touch with the shipping firm Boatwright sailed for. That's what I did today, before I came out here with Swope. I was told Captain Buggins had put into Boston two weeks ago, that he'd delivered his manifest, whatever that may be, gone ashore, and not returned by sailing time, so they promoted the mates and left without him."

Grace Porble gasped. "Didn't anybody even call the police?"

"Oh, no. I gather this is the sort of thing that happens fairly often with that particular line. The owners are more concerned to avoid publicity than to get them back."

"But what if they're being shanghaied?" asked Cronkite Swope, whose imagination ran to the picaresque.

"My impression was that they're more apt to have been picked up by the police for smuggling narcotics. Since Captain Buggins was known to have relatives in the area, they gave him the benefit of the doubt and assumed he'd simply forgotten to mention that he was taking extended shore leave."

"Well, I must say," Grace Porble began.

"Must you really, or can it wait a bit?" her husband interrupted. "Because I do think, dear, that we ought to go and tell Purve and Sephy about this before they hear it from somebody else. Sephy's been through an awfully rough time, and this isn't going to make things any easier for her."

Grace sighed. "You're right, Phil, though I don't think Sephy ever had any illusions about Brace. She was against the lawsuit from the start, but her parents' hearts were so set on it that she couldn't bring herself to stand against them. They'd never had anything, and here was their last chance. And it was going to bring Brace home. They were so excited about that. He'd been away so long, they'd forgotten what he's like. When he called them up and told them about this document he'd discovered—"

"What document?" Helen demanded.

"I don't know. Sephy wouldn't tell me. I'm not sure she knows herself."

"It's a deed of the property from Abelard Buggins to his son Ichabod," Minerva Mink piped up. "I've seen the deed myself. I hope you don't think I'd have been fool enough to get involved in this affair if Bracebridge hadn't been able to prove to me for a positive fact that he was going to win his suit."

"Where is this deed now?" Helen insisted.

"Someplace where you'll never find it, Blondie," snarled Bracebridge.

"Cut the crap, Humphrey Bogart," Marietta Woozle growled back. "It's in his inside coat pocket, in a fake leather passport case."

Chief Ottermole advanced on the prisoner. "Okay, Buggins, I'll take that paper."

"Like hell you will."

"You resisting a police officer in the performance of his duty?"

Ottermole sounded quite pleased to be resisted. He was half a head taller than Bracebridge and a couple of decades younger. Buggins was down and the passport out almost before Cronkite Swope could snap his shutter.

"Here, Professor," said the victor. "You want to read it aloud?"

"He forgot his reading glasses," said Swope eagerly. "Let me."

"Go ahead," said Shandy.

"It's that funny old-time writing and the ink's pretty faded, but I guess I can make it out." Swope cleared his throat.

"I, Abelard Bugginf, prefent the Parcel of Land meafuring one fquare Acre from ye Granite Markerf around Oozakf Pond to my Fon Ichabod on hif 18th

Birthday, thif Land being Won by me in a wager with my Bro. Balaclava Bugginf, who attempted to Beft my Prize Workhorfe Famfon with a Black Nag of hif own breeding in a Pulling Conteft. Let thif be a Warning and an Admonifhment to my Fon never to make a Wager when in Drink Taken. Y^e Balaclava Black came nigh to Winning ye Conteft, in which Cafe I w'd have had to Pay One Thoufand Dollarf into y't Mad Fcheme my Bro. callf hif College.

> By My Hand and Feal,
> Abelard Bugginf

P.F Balaclava waf Drunker than I waf. Elfe he w'd not have Gambled away Land he c'd ill afford to lofe."

"There," said Miss Mink. "You see?"

Dr. Porble took the paper from Swope. "Undated, unfortunately. This does look awfully authentic, President. The paper's old, the ink faded—and Balaclava had waited so long to found his college. The wager could have been a last-ditch attempt to raise some cash."

"No it couldn't," said Helen Shandy. "Ichabod Buggins was born August fourth, 1809, which means he'd have turned eighteen in 1827. Balaclava Buggins had owned other horses, but never a black mare until he bought a filly he called Balaclava Betsy from a farmer named Purvis Mink, interestingly enough, on October second, 1862. He paid ten and a half dollars and didn't have her bred until the following April twenty-second, giving a sack of seed potatoes as the stud fee. So the deed's a fake. I'm sorry, Miss Mink."

"I'm not," said Thorkjeld Svenson. "Ottermole, is my librarian unjugged?"

"Huh? Yeah, sure, Dr. Svenson."

"Then go, Porble. Back to work. You run the library, and let Helen handle the big stuff."

"With pleasure," said the librarian. "Ride back with Grace and me, Harry. It appears we have business to discuss. Unless you need the car, Ottermole?"

"I'll be glad to take the prisoners in the press car," Cronkite Swope offered eagerly. "It'll be another scoop for the *Fane and Pennon*."

> *"'So retribution followed soon*
> *Upon their wicked heels,*
> *For preyful crook should gain no boon*
> *From any pond he steals,'"*

Peter Shandy murmured.

"Come on, President, I don't think the press car's up to your weight. I suggest we take Buggins with us, while Ottermole and Swope escort the ladies. You don't mind driving the car, Helen?"

"Not at all."

But Helen didn't start right away. She sat gazing after the big black car Marietta Woozle had described with such ill-meant accuracy. "So that's who it was. Poor Grace, she's taking it badly, and no wonder. You know, Peter, Corydon Buggins would positively have gone to town on this one."

"He already did," said Shandy. "It's right there in the archives, dear:

> *"'Tho' waterlogged in death, may he*
> *Enjoy a dry Eternity*
> *While still she dwells with mem'ry fond*
> *Upon the corpse in Oozak's Pond.'"*